I0531651

THE CRYSTAL PORTAL

A SUPERHERO ROMANCE

BOOK ONE

NERO'S TOUCH

By Joyce Holland

From the moment Dinah Masters and Nero Lockwood meet, sparks begin to fly. And not only the kind of sparks ignited by romance, but the kind that starts fires. Fighting their burning attraction is out of the question, because they soon learn they can trust no one but each other.

When superheroes are created, they must pick a cause. Dinah chooses one that can change the world, one *little person* at a time. But at every turn they learn secrets hidden for centuries, secrets that come with power they never imagined. And power is a two edged sword, it can kill or cure.

This book is dedicated to all the romantic women in my family. (In alphabetical order) Allison, Amber, Beth, Cassie, Erin, Holly, Karen, Katie, Laura, Penny, Sherry, & Tina. And as always, to my husband, Tony, who actually believes I can write.

A special thanks to Cathy Jones, Graeme Jones, Dr. Alan Menkes, and Lee Thomas, my intrepid editors, for daring to leap into my *make-believe* world.

Merrell & Knapp ~*~ 2013

The Crystal Portal
BOOK ONE
NERO'S TOUCH

A Superhero Romance Trilogy

By

Joyce Holland

CHAPTER ONE

Dinah stopped abruptly and breathed in the crisp mountain air. A deep ravine gaped below her. She forced herself to stare down the tree-covered slope, deliberately challenging her fear of heights.

Nero followed her gaze into the abyss and quickly braced himself against the cliff wall. "In case you hadn't noticed, the path is pretty narrow here. When you plan to stop suddenly, you need to let me know, okay? I can't believe I'm partnered with a woman."

Dinah turned and faced Nero Lockwood.

"Look, Buster, I'm not any happier about it than you. You drew my name, done deal. How do you think I feel? We trek through one of the most magnificent settings on God's Earth and you do nothing but complain. Geez!"

"When I signed up for this trip, I thought it was a guy thing." He countered. "You're right though, it is beautiful. But didn't there used to be some secret laboratory around here somewhere? I can't think of a better way to ruin natural beauty."

She nodded. "Yeah, at last something we agree on. They hid it up here in the mountains thinking a bunch of ignorant moonshiners wouldn't give a hoot. It remained a huge secret until rumors spread regarding a radiation leak. Some sassy senator took on their cause and fought to have it dismantled."

"Hard to believe, a politician helping his constituents."

Dinah smiled. "I know, but I'm so glad he did. It's awesome up here." She waved a hand at the surrounding mountains, the towering pines, and the rock encrusted butte to one side of them on the trail. She flipped her long blond ponytail over one shoulder and raised her face to the breeze. "Let's get moving. I smell water."

Nero uttered a harsh laugh. "What are you, some kind of ruminant?"

"Ruminant?" She stiffened. "What the hell's a ruminant?"

"Don't get your back up. It's just a herd animal that can smell water. You remember in the old westerns where the steers smell a water-hole and all but stampede in their haste to get there?"

Dinah pursed her lips in disapproval. "So, you're calling me a cow?"

He threw up his hands. "If you were a guy, you would have thought the remark funny. I meant it to be." He eyed her from head to foot. "You are definitely not a guy."

"Pfft! The first nice thing you've said to me all day." She laughed and pulled out a map. "And I hope you're a guy with map savvy, because we've strayed a tad from the assigned route."

"Hey, I have a GPS, remember? We can't get lost But I hope you do smell a water-hole because I wouldn't mind cooling off in it."

"Neither would I, but with our luck they probably used it as a runoff for nuclear waste."

He frowned. "I'm sure they weren't allowed to do that."

"Yeah, right. I'm sure social prudence stopped them. And I don't care if you call me a cow again." She sniffed the air once more. "I'll bet we find water on the other side of these rocks." Actually, Dinah knew a pool existed, her physics professor had elaborated on its spectacular beauty. He'd also pleaded with her not to venture near the mountain, no less the pool.

Nero stretched and yawned, and she couldn't help but notice his muscular body. He must work out every day, she thought with appreciation, then derided herself for noticing. He registered in her mind as the typical jock; probably watched himself in gym mirrors when he flexed those gorgeous abs. Nope, she didn't like him. Period. She avoided dark sexy men. When she dated at all, she dated geeks. Brains far outclassed brawn.

"How much or what exactly?"

"Huh? How much what?"

"How much or what will you bet?" He shrugged. "It's a guy thing, betting."

Dinah narrowed her eyes and glared at him, saying nothing.

He made a rude face. "Forget it. I'm not suggesting the stakes be a roll in the hay or anything. Besides, you're not my type."

How dare he. "Oh, really, and what exactly is your type?"

He gave her an evil grin. "Feminine, for starters. And the women I date don't carry thirty-pound packs on their backs and wear hiking boots with steel toes. They don't start fires with sticks or bathe in icy streams."

She fought the urge to push him off the cliff. "Oh yeah, well the men I date don't pose in front of gym mirrors either, or spend more time primping for a date than I do." She saw him redden and knew she had struck a chord. Aha! He did pose in front of those mirrors. Dinah whirled around and marched ahead, not caring if he followed or not.

"Let's call a truce," he hollered from behind her. "This is juvenile."

Dinah's reply caught in her throat as she turned the bend. At last, the beautiful pool Professor Dumas had spoken of, and it appeared ten times more glorious than advertised. The water radiated a strange, almost iridescent violet hue. The sight stunned her. It resembled something she imagined would be found on another planet. She'd never seen water that color. The surface gave off a silky glow that didn't come from reflected sunlight. In fact, a dark cloud obscured the sun at the moment, lending the whole scene an otherworldly aura. It took her breath away.

Apparently, it took Nero's breath away, too, because she heard his quick intake as he drew up alongside her. "My God, I can't believe my eyes. It's surreal."

Together, no longer bantering words, they scampered down the slope to the rock strewn shore. Because they were now in a natural bowl with hills all around them, the breeze had evaporated and the stillness lent an even eerier effect to their surroundings. Perspiration streamed off them and collected in their clothing.

Nero reached down and dipped his hand in the pool. "Wow, it's so hot in this valley, I'm surprised the water stays so cold. It must be really deep, probably spring fed. I said I wouldn't mind taking a dip in the watering hole, but I'm not so sure now, this place gives me the willies."

Dinah bent and checked the water temperature. "It doesn't matter," she announced with a forced air of confidence, "little ole unfeminine me will not be deterred by cool water. I think I'll take a dip." She gave him a sardonic smile. "Just as soon as I shed my steel-toed boots. It's a girl thing." Whereupon, she unceremoniously undressed.

If her actions surprised Nero, it didn't

show because his feelings remained hidden behind a stony façade as he stared at her.

"Hey, take a picture why don't you."

"Sorry, like I said, you are most certainly—not a guy." He gave her a lecherous grin; then he disrobed, too.

Neither went beyond their underwear.

At the last minute, Nero came and stood next to her, head lowered, as though to let her know he felt contrite. "Dinah, I didn't mean to challenge you. You don't have to prove anything, and I never said you weren't feminine. I even think it's sexy that you carry a heavy backpack with ease. Truth be told, I think you are the sexiest woman I've ever seen. Unfortunately, I tend to get snotty when tweaked." He glanced up and changed the subject quickly. "I don't like the look of those bloated clouds hovering overhead; maybe we shouldn't do this. They probably hold lightning."

Dinah blushed at his words, but chose not to respond to them directly. She would weigh them later, for validity and motive, but she

11

managed a polite reply. "Thank you, I think. Look, I know I'm stubborn, I admit it, and I did feel challenged." She smiled faintly. "Problem is, I grew up with two male cousins who never stopped baiting me. I owe them for toughening me up, maybe too much so." She didn't comment on the strange cloud, the particular phenomenon Dumas had cautioned might be dangerous. Strange weather occurrences, he'd said, potentially lethal ones. Surely he exaggerated.

She turned to Nero, "But, here we are, half naked, while you're telling me you think I'm sexy, and I don't know beans about you. One thing is for sure, I would feel a whole lot better under the cover of water!" Without further comment, she plunged in, leaving him little choice but to do likewise.

They'd only swum a few feet when he voiced his fears. "Ah, did you happen to notice there is no *normal* edge to this pool?"

She stopped and treaded water beside him. "What do you mean—no *normal* edge?"

"Precisely what I said. We didn't wade in,

we jumped in. Rather like jumping into a round fish bowl with a small opening, filled to the top. I get the feeling the water goes under the edge of the shore. Do you know what I mean?"

Dinah looked back, at the shore. "You're creeping me out." But she caught his meaning alright. "Do you honestly think it's the same all the way around?" She spun slowly to look.

"I do," he said.

A loud peal of thunder cut off further conversation.

Instinctively, Dinah reached for him and he took her into his arms. They were inches apart. She didn't know if it was the fear she felt, the need for comfort, or him calling her sexy, but when he kissed her, she kissed him back. Big time.

That's when the bolt of lightning struck the pool. The water turned from violet to deep purple and shimmered as though an earthquake had troubled it. A low humming noise echoed across the small valley and spread to the base of the encompassing mountains.

Suddenly, a fierce ribbon of pain traveled the length of Dinah's body, and the kiss became a fusion point from which neither could escape. A burst of unearthly power rocketed between and through them. The air above them became a misty greenish cloud. The greenish cloud that Professor Dumas mentioned. *Oh no, she should have listened.* Another bolt of lightning struck the pool. Dinah felt herself go fuzzy for a heartbeat, and in that heartbeat something changed for both of them. Forever.

~*~

Dinah gasped for air and drew in a mouthful of water. She tried to recall what had happened. Water, she floated in water. The pool. The lightning. Nero and the kiss. The cloud. She went under again and struggled to surface. She gasped for air once more and then saw Nero less than two feet away.

He stayed away. "Thank God," he said. "I thought you would never come to."

Couldn't he see she was drowning? "Why are we still in the pool?"

He didn't answer. Instead he studied the clouds overhead.

His expression frightened her as did something else. "Nero, your hair has turned completely red!"

"I couldn't get you out of the pool, and my hair is the least of our problems."

"You can't get me out? What about yourself? Can you get out?"

"I can and I did, but every time I tried to tug you to shore, I shocked us both. You cried out and I worried you would continue to pass out."

Dinah kicked her legs to keep herself upright and glanced around. They were right next to the edge of the pool and she could see beneath the surface of the land. He was right about it being a fishbowl. The water stretched away under the land and she couldn't see the bottom. She shivered with fear. "Please, please, Nero, get me out of here."

"Calm down, I will, now that you're conscious. I'm going to crawl out and get something for you to hold onto." He grasped the rough surface of the rock strewn shore and hauled himself up unto his belly, then threw one leg over and edged up onto dry land.

Dinah grimaced. "I don't think I can do that,"

"Just be still, I'll get my shirt and pull you out."

"Hurry. This water feels alive. Help! It's tugging on my legs." She sank beneath the surface.

"Dinah! He screamed as she popped back up. He made a mad dash for their clothing and something to toss to her.

She sobbed loudly now, terrified of she knew not what.

He returned with his shirt and extended it out as far as he dared without falling back in himself. "Grab hold, quickly, the water is starting to churn. I think it's a whirlpool.

"Oh, my God! Oh, my God!" The sucking

sound of the whirlpool muffled her screams. She reached out and grabbed the shirt just in time and Nero dragged her over the jagged shoreline and a few feet across the stones. She looked back and saw the water swirling wildly for a moment. Then it slowly returned to the nice peaceful pool of only moments before. She collapsed on the bank. Overhead she saw a small cloud descending. She could swear it pulled at her, like gravity, drawing her back toward the pool.

"Get up quick!" he bellowed, "We need to grab our things and get away from here."

Taking his point, Dinah reached for her pack, bounded to her feet and tried to run, but the pull continued. She fought against it. "I can hardly move my feet, something is trying to pull me back to the pool."

Nero cried out. "Come on, run! You can do it, you have to!"

She lost ground; then suddenly broke free with such force she almost fell on the rocks. Gasping with relief, she ran behind him up the side of the hill, wanting to put as much space between them and the pool as possible.

Once back on the mountain trail, they panted heavily and looked at each other. Dinah read the terror reflected in his expression. She turned away, afraid to see more. They slid to a sitting position against the rock wall and as soon as their strength returned, pulled their clothing back on.

Dressed again and feeling only slightly more secure, Dinah announced. "Do not, I repeat, do not ever kiss me again," she said and burst out laughing.

He turned at her inappropriate response. "Oh, oh, you're hysterical, or in shock, more likely." He grabbed a blanket from his pack and tossed it to her. "I'd wrap you up, but…" He left the problem unspoken.

Her laughter turned into tears and her tears into loud sobs. Taking the proffered blanket she wrapped it around her shoulders. "What the hell happened back there?" She finally managed to choke out. "Even after I left the pool, I think the cloud tried to drag me back."

"I don't have the foggiest idea, but I have a feeling you might. We were off our mapped route for over an hour, I have the GPS remember? You knew where we were going. I just wanted to see what you were up to. I realized we had entered the restricted area and I simply decided you were quite adventurous. Actually I've snuck up here a few times on my own over the years, but I've never heard anyone mention a lake or pool. You knew it was up here didn't you, and that there was something strange about it?"

Dinah struggled to regroup. "Not that strange!" She shook her head. "Do you honestly believe I would have jumped in if I did?" She became pensive as she studied him. "I wasn't kidding when I said your hair has turned red, bright red."

"Yeah, I believe you"

"You do?"

He gave her a lopsided grin. "Yes, because so has yours."

"No way!" Dinah snatched her errant ponytail from behind her head to where she could examine it. "Good grief! It's red."

"I could have sworn I just said that. So tell me what you know about the pool and its strange powers. Does the color of the water have anything to do with it?"

"No, the strangeness doesn't have anything to do with the water—at least I don't think so. It has to do with weird weather patterns in this area, seriously, local things no one can explain. You saw the funny cloud hovering like a ghost waiting to pounce?" She fixed him with her sternest look. "And I'm telling you, it *did* try to grab me! Anyway, my physics professor told me about it."

"But you have to admit," Nero interrupted. "The color of the pool begs an explanation. Did your professor give one?"

"According to Doctor Dumas, the color comes from mineral deposits lining the bottom of the pool. He didn't mention its depth or that it was hollow under the shore." She resolved to forget that scary recollection and prayed to not have dreams about it. Besides, people-snatching-clouds made the pool's threat pale in significance. "It's the lightning and green clouds the scientists find interesting. It's just a coincidence we were in the water when it struck."

"Really? Then why the sudden whirlpool? It almost sucked you down! If you ask me, the pool was after you."

Dinah shuddered. "I felt a tremor when we kissed, maybe a small quake is responsible; they happen a lot in this part of the country."

"What, my fabulous kissing ability doesn't get credit for the tremor?"

Dinah smacked him on the arm and recoiled as sparks erupted between them. She screeched in alarm. "What the hell."

"Don't say I didn't warn you. The same thing happened every time I touched you in the water."

Dinah rapped her head lightly against the rock wall as though trying to knock some sense into it. Doc Dumas, or Dumma, as she had called him since she was a child, had a lot of questions to answer. Of course, he had told her to stay away from the area in the first place, but he should have known she would take the warning as a dare.

Nero waved his hand in front of her face. "Earth to Dinah. Don't panic, but someone is watching us."

The other thing she hadn't mentioned. Dumma said government agents monitored the place from time to time. No need for Nero to know every detail, at least not right now. "It's probably some of the other hikers," she said.

"Not this far off track, it's not," he said with a frown. "I don't know about you, but I'm feeling a little odd all of a sudden, like my muscles are bunching up, maybe going to cramp or something. You okay?"

She considered his question. She did feel different, but she couldn't pin down what *different* meant in her case. "My muscles don't feel bunchy at all, in fact they feel light, as though I could drift off the ground. Totally weird." She threw her hands in the air in exasperation—and rose a foot in the air.

Nero grasped the hem of her shorts and pulled her down.

For the first time in her life, Dinah was speechless. As she settled back to Earth she sat there with a blank expression.

Nero regained her attention by waving his hand in front of her eyes again. "We have to face it, whatever happened back there in the lightning...it changed us. When I said a minute ago that someone was watching us, I didn't see *them*, I saw *them* watching us, through their eyes. I can see what they see." He rubbed his palms beneath his eyes until his cheeks were almost as red as his hair. We need to get off this mountain and to a place where we can figure out what's going on."

Dinah remained frozen.

"Dinah, snap out of it."

"I'm trying, really I am. Give me a minute." She wanted to have Nero hold her again, to cover her with kisses so she wouldn't float away. Besides, she'd never experienced an all-consuming kiss like that before, a kiss she had waited for all her life. A kiss of fate. *And why did such a stupid thought enter her feeble brain at a time like this?* One minute she hated this guy, the next she lusted after his touch, and his touch electrified her. The lightning had addled her brain. She stared into his deep dark eyes—and reached for him. *Who cared why?* "Hold me, Nero," she pleaded.

He held up one hand. "Whoa, the shocks, it might hurt, even knock us out."

"What if we can never touch anyone again, never hold a child in our arms, never make love to someone? We have to find out." A tear ran down her cheek. She extended her hands toward him, palms up. "Please, try."

He hesitated for a moment; then placed his hands inches above hers.

Dinah saw small sparks pass between them. Goosebumps rose on her forearms. Risking the worst, she latched onto him. The voltage charge shook them both and they suddenly couldn't let go. It was like the kiss, they were fused together, but this time the charge slowly dissipated. Perhaps they had only needed to release the pent up energy. Dinah sighed as the shocks were replaced with a warm glow, it started where their hands met and traveled to all corners of her being. She wondered if he felt it, too.

He must have because he suddenly pulled her into his arms and covered her face with kisses, as though having read her thoughts of a minute ago. His hands caressed her back, her neck. Then, just as suddenly, he pulled away. "They're coming," he said, "They're coming fast. Agents, whatever that means. No wait, I know— government agents. Can you run?"

"I think I can do even better. Let's see." She threw her arms around him once more and they lifted several feet off the ground. She couldn't even feel her own weight, no less his. They were like feathers on the wind. *But could they really fly this way?* Did they have a choice? "Grab the packs, she instructed, we have IDs in them."

Nero snatched up their things, careful to leave nothing behind. They were officially on the run, or in this case, on the fly.

"Any ideas on where we should go," she asked, pressing her mouth near his ear as they rose into the air.

"Wow! We're flying. I can't concentrate at a moment like this. Okay, okay! I'm adjusting. Ah…I have a small hunting lodge not far from here, it's not totally remote, but it's certainly off the beaten track. Very few people know about it. We could go there for a day or two without anyone knowing, although I do have a friend who uses it on occasion, a writer who feels he has to get away to be creative. Today's Monday. I keep it pretty well supplied so we should be good for several days. He rarely comes on weekdays. Why, did you have a particular destination in mind?" He asked, holding on for dear life as they cleared the treetops.

"Yes, to see Professor Dumas. I think it's time for him to entertain us with the answers to some questions I have. But that can wait until we regroup and get a handle on our situation." Dinah narrowed her eyes and frowned. "I particularly want to know if his hair has always been bright red."

CHAPTER TWO

Dinah looked down as they passed the hiker's drop off area. "The only cool thing about this is I've totally lost my fear of heights. I can't fall." She stifled a giggle. "I know it's probably kind of scary, but could you look down and tell me how we get to this cabin of yours?"

"Do I have to? Just kidding." He pointed. "If you follow the highway north for five or so miles you'll see a bright flashing sign on a tavern called Big Bertha's. There's a dirt track about a mile past it, turn east and follow it another five miles. It dead ends at the cabin."

"Hold on, I'm going to try and go really fast to cut the chances of someone seeing us. I'll keep as far away from the highway as I can without losing sight of it." Their speed tripled suddenly, then quadrupled. She tried to look at him for a reaction. "Of course, if I saw two people flying, I'm not sure I'd report it, they'd lock me in the loony bin. On the other hand, I hope someone does see us and takes a picture. It might be fun to be on the front page of one of those supermarket tabloids."

Dinah felt him tighten his grip as he spoke into her ear. "You're a goofball, you know that? But you're a sexy goofball. Anyway, do you realize that less than two hours ago we could hardly speak without snapping at each other and here we are body to body, flying across the late afternoon sky? Is this romantic or what?"

"I refuse to answer." She smiled, but knew he couldn't see it. "And to think, I could have been paired with the gorgeous hunk sporting the crew cut." She squinted into the wind. "I see the flashing sign on the tavern."

"Huh? No way. It has to be several miles ahead."

"It is, apparently the flying ability comes coupled with eagle-eye vision."

"Hey, not fair. All I got was the ability to see into people's heads."

"Maybe that's not all, you said your muscles were bunching up, maybe you have super strength or something. We have a lot to learn, I think."

They landed hard in front of the cabin, so hard Dinah worried she might have seriously injured Nero, but he sprang to a standing position faster than she did.

"Are you okay?"

He brushed himself off and stomped his feet a few times, probably to see if they still worked, she thought.

"I'll live."

"Personally," she said with a smile, "I

think I did rather well for a first landing."

He raised one eyebrow.

"Okay, so I need to practice a little, I'll do better next time." She turned to face the cabin. "Nice place you have here, very rustic. I love it! I can't wait to see the inside."

He walked over to some bushes and retrieved the keys from a small box hidden near the roots. "It's not exactly posh inside, but it's comfortable." He led the way up the steps to the porch that stretched the length of the building. Rocking chairs were scattered here and there and a hammock graced one end.

"I've never been in a real log cabin," she said as they entered. The door opened onto a great-room. A small kitchen sat at the back, complete with a breakfast bar that separated it from the main room. Above, a loft covered three walls and she noticed curtains divided it into sections. "Where's the bathroom?" She asked, envisioning a tiny building out back with a half-moon cut into the door. "Please don't tell me it's outside."

He grinned. "Yes and no. This place is so old it used to have an outhouse, but I added a bathroom on." He indicated the far wall near the kitchen. "Over there. You can't see it from outside because it's tacked on the back of the cabin, but don't worry, it has all the modern conveniences, even a small hot tub."

"Perfect." She made a bee-line for the bathroom door. "I assume it has a mirror, I have to see my hair!"

To her credit, she screamed only once, loud and mournfully.

Once past the initial shock of her hair, she wandered through the cabin checking out the furnishings, which were sparse. Two overstuffed couches sat sideways, facing each other near the giant fireplace and a leather recliner sat in a corner by itself with only a pole lamp for company. The center of the room held a huge scarred oak table and eight chairs dotted its circumference. "Do you hold meetings here or something?"

"It's a camp for enjoying the great

outdoors. I often bring a bunch of buddies up here and we hunt and play cards and stuff. It's more like a bunkhouse really. In fact, you'll find four bunk beds upstairs."

"This is a pretty big place, and if you don't live here, you must be rich to have this and a home, too." She frowned. "I'm just curious, are you? Rich, I mean?"

"In my dreams. No, my great-great-grandfather owned it. He built it almost a hundred years ago, and it passed to my dad and then to me—when he died."

"Sorry about your dad, but why would your great-great whatever build out here in the middle of nowhere?"

"He trapped for a living, beaver mostly. A dozen or more streams intersect the property, they come down out of the mountains we hiked in today. Anyway, it will all go to my son one of these days."

"You have a son?" It had not occurred to Dinah he might have children, no less a wife. She felt herself pale. *She had kissed the hell out of him, and he might be married?*

"Not yet," he said with a wry grin. "First I need to find a wife. Well, in today's world, perhaps not, but I'm the old fashioned type. I believe in marriage."

"Oh!" She sputtered, amazed at the level of relief his words provided. "So, let's get down to business."

He nodded in agreement. "Right. I'm going to pop some frozen dinners in the microwave and grab a couple of beers. How does that sound?" He didn't wait for an answer, just moved toward the fridge. "We can talk while we eat. I don't know about you, but I'm suddenly starved. I hope you like spaghetti."

"Love it. Do you keep any red wine on hand?"

"A bottle of Chianti does sound better."

CHAPTER THREE

Dinah finished the last of her spaghetti and sampled another sip of wine. "Are we like those superheroes in the comic books now? You know, Superman, Spiderman, other worldly?"

"I haven't a clue, but I think we need to find out exactly what we can do in terms of special powers. And if you recall, those superheroes you mentioned, were fictional. And the operative word was 'heroes.' Having super powers doesn't necessarily make one heroic. Being a superhero would require dedicating oneself to helping mankind. You ready to sign

35

on?"

"As far as I know, all I can do is fly. Lord, even saying it aloud sounds weird, and why do I accept it so easily. You'd think I would be overcome with shock at the very idea of flying. What else has changed in my psyche? I should be scared spitless. I'm not."

"I know. I felt the same way about being in those guys' heads. It should have given me a heart attack, but it felt perfectly natural. One minute I'm an ordinary guy, and the next thing I know I'm a mind reader." He frowned. "Well, not a mind reader per se, because I couldn't read their thoughts, but I could see through their eyes and hear their words. I felt like a mini video camera hiding in their heads and looking out. It's hard to explain." He sighed loudly. "How can we test to see what other aspects of our lives are affected?"

"Those powers came unbidden. I floated up and you dropped into someone else's brain. Which brings up another question. Did they know you were there? Is that why they zeroed in on us? And what made you go to them."

"Good question, and I have part of the answer. I remember experiencing a sudden sense of danger, much like anyone feels when they say they have the feeling they are being watched, only a hundred times stronger in my case. The minute I felt it I *reached*, there's no other way to describe it—I *reached*."

"Awesome."

"Personally, I'd rather fly. But let's start at the beginning. What does your professor friend know about these oddities?"

"Apparently, a lot more than he's told me. He's my mentor, and a family friend, but he's more like a father to me. My parents had me quite late in life, which is why I gravitate toward older people, I guess, and he's quite old—at least I think he is. I've never asked him how old he is, he's just…mature. I have no other family to speak of, both my cousins died in the war, and my parents are in a home. They barely know me most of the time. I've made him my family these last ten years. And since I grew up knowing him, it seemed natural. Anyway, he had a little too much wine one night at my house and started talking really weird." She frowned in remembrance.

"He actually was one of the scientists who worked at the secret laboratory. He lived on the property as did many of them. And, he used to swim in the crystal portal, that's what he called the pool. Beyond vague recollections of other people, one, a woman named Nadine, he just babbled on and on about her and other things I didn't understand, physics and alien phenomena he saw during his years there. I figured he was hallucinating from the overabundance of alcohol. Then he went into detail on the weather thing, insisting it was dangerous. I thought he exaggerated when he mentioned green clouds and star portals and such. And mostly I passed it off as an old man embellishing a story, except for when he waxed eloquent regarding the pool. His vivid description fascinated me and I knew I had to get there one day. Now I wish I had recorded everything he said."

Nero nodded. "In a day or two, we should contact him and meet him somewhere so we can talk."

Dinah suddenly stood up. "Speaking of the pool and our little adventure, we didn't sign out at the hiking checkpoint, they might be looking for us. Should we call someone?

"No, I vote against calling for the moment. I suspect those government agents know exactly who we are right now, for that very reason. If the camp owner reported us missing, it wouldn't take a genius to figure out we were the trespassers."

"Right, ah…I failed to mention one little thing. The professor did say government agents patrol the area. Even you know it's off limits to hikers because they claim there might still be some hotspots from the leak years ago, although they've never come out and actually said so.

"Anyway, they let the rumors persist and claim they use the area for military exercises, but there isn't a military installation within 50 miles of here." She raised a hand to stop his obviously rising protest. "Dumas also said there was never, ever a leak, just a rumor of one, but the senator used the fabrication to close them down to make a name for himself. I wouldn't expose myself or anyone to radiation, honest. I merely wanted to swim in a crystal pool." She sat back down and rested her head on her hands. "You're right, I am a goofball."

"I said you were a *sexy* goofball, big difference" He reached for her hand and sparks flew. "Damn, here we go again." He snatched his hand away.

Dinah couldn't help but laugh, but recovered quickly after seeing his hurt expression. "I'm sorry I didn't tell you about the agents. But that's before we flew away together. Dear God, I'm talking about flying as though everyone did it." She tapped her nails on the table. "If we don't call, won't they send out search teams?"

"Let me give it some thought. The problem is, if we call, the agents will dog us because they know a whole lot more about the place than we do. Something odd is still going on up there for them to be monitoring it for thirty years. And, with them dogging us it's going to be hard to become superheroes." His grin was infectious.

"Wow! Superheroes. You mean it? Wouldn't that be something?" She grinned back. "Hmmm…If you really wanted to become a superhero what kind would you be?"

"Is there more than one kind?" He shook his head. "Weren't they all dedicated to combating evil and helping mankind?"

"Yeah, there's the rub. Why become *ordinary* superheroes? I propose we specialize in certain types of evil."

"I see, so we really have decided to be superheroes, have we? That's what it sounds like from where I sit." He leaned back in his chair and studied her, his expression reflecting the pertinent question.

She brightened. "Why not? I can fly and you can 'reach.' What a duo we'd make." She paused and pursed her lips. "Children, little children. A super duo who extend themselves for those most vulnerable. We could set up a website for people to contact us, maybe even the children themselves, most of them practically live on the Internet. In our day, we played with the bells and whistles on Fischer Price toys. Kids today google *dinosaur dot com* on their smart phones."

He looked heavenward and clasped his hands together. "Help me, Lord," he pleaded. "I think I'm falling in love with a goofball."

She copied his actions. "And I think I'm falling in love with him, too, Lord, but I'm not going to sleep with him until I'm sure."

Nero dropped his hands to the table. "Well, we certainly cleared up that unspoken question nicely. Thank you very much, now I won't have to suffer the insult of personal rejection. But I can live with that. And speaking of sleeping–I need a kiss goodnight. Brace yourself." He reached out and touched her hand.

After the initial shock wore off, he pulled her onto his lap and held her to his chest and kissed her wildly.

Inwardly, Dinah wondered if what they experienced was as much a result of their bizarre circumstances as it was their highly charged physical attraction, but as his hands explored her with abandon, she realized, she didn't care. Never in her life had she felt such rising passion for anyone. If they kept this up much longer, her hastily made resolution would weaken, if not fail.

"Turn around and straddle me," he whispered in her ear. "We don't have to do anything. I can't hold you close enough this way."

"I…" She started to protest, then did as he asked. Now they were body to body in the most intimate way and Dinah's every nerve screamed for more. She felt as though the air around them might ignite from their combined heat. His kisses set her adrift on a hormonal sea. A shaky moan escaped her lips and he smothered it with his own.

"Nero?" A loud voice proclaimed from the suddenly opened front door.

"Rafael!" Nero rocked back, nearly

dumping Dinah on the floor as he stood.

"I'm really, really sorry to interrupt. I didn't know you were here." Rafael whirled around and faced the yard, as though to give them time to regroup.

"How'd you get here?" Rafael asked the outside world. "There's no car out front. I got nervous when I discovered the keys missing. I thought maybe kids had found them or something. He faced them again. "And what the hell happened to your hair? You look freaky."

"I flew in." Nero said with a laugh. "Just kidding. Actually, a friend brought me and dropped me out front."

Dinah snickered.

She straightened her shorts and tucked in her blouse. When had it come untucked? She made a quick analysis of the man in the doorway. He was male-model handsome, with dark hair and eyelashes enviously longer than hers. Unfair. His hooded brows suggested a brooding nature, but his smile told a different story, it reflected an innocent boyish demeanor.

"I have a deadline for my new book and you told me to come up here and write any time I wanted, so here I am." He removed his hat, but didn't hang it on the rack, clearly undecided about staying. "I though you went trekking in the mountains."

"Long story—short trek. Anyway, it's good to see you. As for my hair, it's temporary." He turned to Dinah, "Excuse my manners, this is Dinah."

Rafael smiled as though relieved of having to explain further. "And I am Rafael Zapata. You're a welcome surprise. I didn't even know Nero was dating anyone, and I've *never* known him to bring a woman here. You must be very important to him. Look, I can just go back home and give you love-birds some privacy."

"No, no," Dinah insisted, shaking her head. "Don't worry, we're not sleeping together."

Nero turned several shades of red. "Gee, Dinah, thanks for sharing that bit of news with my best friend." To Rafael he said with a smile. "She comes off a little blunt sometimes."

Dinah opened her mouth to object, but thought better of it. She smiled brightly back at him. "Have any more wine, sweetheart? Please persuade Rafael to join us." She fetched another glass from the kitchen area and placed it on the table.

Rafael stood still, and a deep frown crossed his face. "Why do I get the feeling you two are talking over my head? I think we'd all be best served if I executed a disappearing act."

"Nonsense, Rafael. Come in, come in, have some wine. You hungry? I can zap another dinner in a heartbeat."

"I ate on the way up." He appeared conflicted. "You're sure I'm not intruding?'

"Positive, go stash your stuff upstairs and I'll open another bottle of vino."

"We should tell him everything," Nero whispered as soon as Rafael climbed the stairs out of earshot.

They heard him murmuring as he opened and closed drawers a bit more dramatically than seemed necessary. "I'm going to take a quick shower," he announced loudly from the balcony, then stomped down the stairs and headed for the attached bathroom in the back.

"He's overdoing it a bit," Nero suggested.

"Are you crazy? What do you mean, tell him everything? What kind of secret superheroes tell everything to the first person they see after receiving their super-duper powers?"

"Smart ones in this case. Do you know anything about computers? Can you set up the Internet site we will need to be sure no one can trace us? Did you have someone in mind to help us do that?"

"When you put it so succinctly... Okay, no, to all of the above. You know this guy well enough, huh?"

"We went to grade school together; I'd trust him with my life."

"Good, because I have a gut feeling that's exactly what you'll be doing. And my life also lies in the balance, remember? I take it he knows computers then?"

"When he's not writing books, it's what

he does, he builds them for customers. He's a computer genius."

"His books, what genre does he write, technical manuals for software?"

"Oh, oh, the important question. He writes science fiction."

She threw her hands in the air. "Naturally, I should have guessed. All right, what the heck, tell him." She glanced toward the kitchen. "Oh boy, here he comes. Pour him some wine, he's going to need it."

CHAPTER FOUR

Rafael proved a good listener. It took thirty minutes to cover everything and the whole time he maintained a blank expression.

Finished, Dinah and Nero waited for his reaction.

Rafael tipped his head to one side as though in deep thought. "I gather this is a book you two are working on. As a pitch, it's rather on the long side and I don't get the sense you have an ending in mind yet, but it has real possibilities. Am I right?

Dinah and Nero looked at each other with stunned expressions.

Dinah spoke first. "Rafael, you just met me, but trust me, everything we just told you really happened. From what Nero tells me, you *do* trust him, so surely you'll believe him. Tell your friend it's true, Nero."

Nero smirked. "It's true, Rafe."

Rafael poured himself some more wine. "If you're playing a joke on me, I'm going to end up majorly pissed off. Retribution will follow."

"It appears drastic measures are called for. Show him, Dinah."

She sighed, figuring it would come to this from the start, and she couldn't blame Rafael. Who would believe such a scenario? She got up from the table and rose to the balcony level of the room.

"Holy shit!" Rafael bellowed. "Your girlfriend is possessed!"

"I am not!" Dinah came down too fast and landed in a heap near the fireplace.

Rafael sprang to his feet. "Are you all

right?"

Dinah stood quickly and nodded. "I'm fine, really I am."

"She needs to practice her landing techniques." Nero contributed. He gave her a thumbs-up sign. "Not bad for a second try, Dinah."

"He called me possessed, it put me off my mark."

Rafael looked from one to the other of them. "If I go back outside and come in again, can I pretend this was all a dream?" He shook his head as he answered his own question. "No, I saw what I saw. So it's all true, the story you told me. And you did fly here. Good Lord. What should we do?"

"Now you're talking, because here's where you come in." Nero explained their idea about the website.

"The website is a cinch and I'd be more than happy to contribute my expertise," Rafael agreed. "My real concern is the agents. They're not going to forget today's shenanigans. Right now I imagine they believe you to still be in the mountains somewhere. But it won't be long before they start looking farther afield." He nodded at Nero. "Armed with a computer, I could find out everything about you in less time than it takes to order a pizza. They will have the resources to do likewise. And once they find out you have this place, it won't be long before they land on your doorstep."

Dinah twisted her hands together. "If they decide to search for me, they won't have to go far, everyone knows I'm closer than family to Professor Dumas. He's going to worry something has happened to me. I should at least call him." She went to retrieve her cell phone from her backpack.

"No! Wait, don't call." Nero yelled. "As a matter of fact, we should turn our cell phones off. They can be used as tracking devices." He ran for his backpack and rummaged through it for his. "I say we remove the batteries, now."

"But the professor…I'm all he has. I don't want to scare him to death. He hasn't been in the greatest of health lately." Dinah placed her phone on the counter as though it were a hand grenade.

Rafael spoke up. "Okay, let's clean this place up like we haven't been here. No garbage, take it with us. I'll drive us into town and rent you a hotel room for now. No more flying for a while, it's too risky. And I'll purchase several cell phones with limited time on them. You can call your professor friend, swear him to secrecy and arrange to meet him in a few days."

Nero peered out the window. "It rained yesterday, you will have left car tracks."

"So, I'll just say I came up here to write for a few hours." Rafael glanced around, "but I didn't use three glasses for wine."

Two hours later Nero, Dinah and Rafael were tucked away in the *Alpine Inn* on the edge of town. The A-framed office was white stucco with dark wood trim, designed to make it look like a chalet. A dubious effort at best. They'd selected it because the designated parking places reposed directly in front of each unit, which meant they didn't have to pass the front desk to access their room. The room itself had the usual mass produced art on the walls and a mini fridge and microwave in one corner. Dinah pronounced it seedy, but adequate.

Rafael handed Dinah one of the newly purchased cell phones. "Make your call, but keep it short and to the point. When you're done I'll take the phone with me and dump it somewhere in case they trace his incoming calls."

Dinah accepted the proffered phone. "This feels like a *Mission Impossible* episode. I think we might have over-reacted, guys." She dialed the professor's home number.

He answered on the second ring.

"Professor Dumas."

"It's me, Dinah. I don't know if they've reported me missing yet or not, but I wanted you to know I'm not lost in the wilderness."

"I'm sorry, young lady. I've discovered I

don't really need them today, but I appreciate your offer to deliver. Something has come up; a dear friend is lost. Why don't I just come by tomorrow to pick up the prescription. I can be there around ten as usual."

"Oh, my God, they're already there, aren't they?"

"Yes, that will be fine, thank you. I'm really must get off the phone, I'm hoping for a call from my missing friend. Goodbye."

"Sir, don't hang up!" A man's voice instructed in the background.

Dinah whirled to face Nero. "Someone was telling him not to hang up, but he did. Do you think they had time to trace it?"

"No," Rafael answered for him. "But his phone records will tell them it was a cell phone— and where the tower that transmitted it is located."

"He pretended it was his pharmacy on the line. They're just around the corner from here, it might be okay."

"It will have to be, I don't think it's wise

to move again right now." Nero sat down heavily on one of the two queen sized beds. "What exactly did he say?"

"He did manage to get me a cryptic message of sorts. Said he would meet me as usual tomorrow at ten, which I translate to mean he would see me at a coffee house we go to near the mall. He walks there with a group of senior citizens every morning and I join him for coffee afterwards."

"Rafael will take your place tomorrow, in case they have agents following Dumas. You can compose a long letter to him tonight and Rafael will deliver it." He motioned for her to sit beside him. "Don't look so troubled, you'll see him again. We'll make a viable plan, I promise."

She leaned her head on his shoulder and sparks flew between them. "Aggrr… Must we go through this every few minutes?"

Rafael choked out a laugh. "Hey, we need to create a grounding system for the two of you."

"Not a half-bad idea," Dinah said. "The professor would know how, he's a genius, literally."

"Give me the phone you used, Dinah. I'm going to get rid of it."

She handed it over. "Don't leave us. When will you return? Are you going home? They may be trying to contact you, too."

"First I'm going to buy you two some hair-dye. I know your color, Nero, but what color was yours, Dinah?"

"Blond, pale blond, but I kind of like this color, it's growing on me. I'll stick with it for now."

"I'll consider the dye," Nero chimed in. He walked over to the mirror.

"Great, now let's start thinking about your superhero costumes." Rafael smiled. "Please consider red. Or yellow. Bye, I'll see you in the morning. I've got a key. I'll let myself in quietly around 9:30, so don't panic when I enter, and ah…wear clothing." He winked.

"*Red and yeller kill a feller*," Dinah quoted to his departing back, recalling the old adage regarding poisonous snakes. "And we're not about killing, we're going to be the good guys. Blue and green is perfect. Which do you want, Nero?

"Green, lime green. And yours should be periwinkle blue." Nero said with enthusiasm. "I know a Vietnamese tailor, he's a confirmed hermit and I think we can swear him to secrecy. But what about masks?"

"Dinah grinned. "I'm up to that one. I did a lot of design work in college, especially when I worked in the drama club. Leave it to me. In fact I have a sketchbook in my backpack, I'll get right on it first thing in the morning." She pointed to the bed nearest the bathroom, once more resolved not to sleep with Nero. "I want that one, and I'm sleeping alone." Lust did not qualify as love, and his closeness made such a distinction difficult to maintain.

~*~

Dinah rose early, dressed, retrieved her sketchpad and some charcoal pencils and moved to the mirror at the counter near the bathroom. She cleared away the toiletries and spread out her supplies. The overhead lights weren't great, but they proved better than the small light over the desk. She turned to where Nero still lay on the bed watching her. "Hmmm...the fun part begins. I don't suppose you would like something feathery, like Mardi Gras masks?

He threatened her with a scowl. "I would not! Something manly if you don't mind." He got up to freshen his coffee from the pot Dinah had made.

"Humph! What do we call ourselves? Superheroes have names like Superman and Wonder Woman."

"What's wrong with Nero?"

"What were your parents thinking anyway? Was your mother a history nut? If so, surely she was aware that Nero laughed while Rome burned."

"Apparently you don't know your history any better than my mother did. He fiddled, not laughed. And my mother wouldn't know Nero from Nefertiti. She did read a lot though, genre mysteries, and guess who her favorite author was? Rex Stout—hence the name. He wrote the Nero Wolfe mystery series. Hey, we could be Nero and Nefertiti."

Dinah had to laugh. "I do like her costume, and I might use her makeup. Lots of eyelashes and classy bangs. But how about Nadya for my name, it's Russian and it means hope. On the other hand, Dinah means justified. I think I'll keep my name. I can look up Nero for you if you like.

"No, don't bother, it means powerful, which works just fine for a superhero. And on the mask, I don't want my mouth covered, make it more like Batman's, without the pointy ears please. Just cover my hair and rim my eye sockets. And we both need capes to match.

"Perfect." She sketched some preliminary ideas, then tore them up and started over. "Are we no longer Nero and Dinah as regular people then? Do we cease to exist?" She covered her face with her hands. "Am I gone?"

Nero wrapped his arms around her shoulders from behind as she leaned over the sketchpad. Sparks flew, but not as violently as before. "I don't know. We could go back to the mountains and say we were just lost for a while."

Rafael walked through the door as Nero finished his sentence. "Afraid not." He tossed several packages on the nearest bed. "Your hair-dye, hats, and some new duds to make you look 'different.' Time to turn the television on. Any local station will do. The sheriff has launched a search for you."

Nero grabbed the remote.

"...young couple is feared lost in the restricted area of the Calique Mountains." A *disembodied voice announced from the TV speakers. "It's not clear why they were there, since it's patrolled regularly to keep people out because of a radiation leak from a weapons laboratory years ago. Although it's forbidden territory, trekkers have been known to sneak into the area to swim in a mountain spring that has taken its share of*

lives over the years. The underground river that feeds the spring is hundreds of feet down and often backs up creating a whirlpool, swallowing the bodies, only some of which turn up twenty or thirty miles downstream. Others are never found. While it's not certain Dinah Masters and Nero Lockwood entered this pool, there is no sign of them either. More on this later as the search continues. Now we turn to our weather...."

Nero pushed the mute button. "Not good."

"I knew we should have reported in," Dinah said as she paced up and down in front of the now silent television.

Rafael raised a hand in protest. "Let's think this through. If those really are federal agents, you might be better off with totally new identities. Otherwise they'll want to question you since there can be no doubt you trespassed yesterday. What if Dinah accidentally drifts into the air while they're watching? They'll lock her up in another kind of laboratory. Hell, they'll probably dissect her."

"That thought occurred to me yesterday." Nero confirmed. He glanced at Dinah. "You're right, we can't be us anymore, and we can't even tell our closest friends. We're going to have to create our own version of the government's witness protection program. Only we'll be protecting ourselves from them."

Rafael interrupted before Dinah could answer. "I can help with that on the Internet. In the meantime, it's almost time for me to meet the professor. Do I just look for an elderly man, or do you have a photo by any chance?"

Dinah dug though her wallet. "Here." She presented him with a picture they had taken at a fairground recently.

"And what's going to make him trust me? He's not likely to take my word just because I tell him I know you."

Dinah thought for a moment. She undid the clasp on the chain she wore around her neck. A gold coin hung from it. "Wear this, and be sure he sees it. He's very intuitive, he'll know I sent you. He gave it to me; it's one of a kind. Don't ask me what kind; I assume it's a foreign coin by the funny symbols on it."

Nero cautioned. "Check out time is 11:00 and I think we should get out of town once you meet with him. We'll be ready to go the minute you get back."

~*~

Dinah reached into one of the bags Rafael brought them, and screeched. "He has to be kidding!" For Dinah, Rafael had chosen a plain grey smock and apron, much like those worn by food service people or maids. For Nero, she pulled out a large white coverall a painter might wear, along with a matching baseball cap.

Nero whistled. "Is Rafael good or what?"

"Or what, if you ask me.' Dinah grimaced. "How soon can you call your tailor friend, I want my superhero suit."

"And I can't wait to measure you. Come

here." When she backed away, he went after her. "Every curve," he continued, "These are going to be form-fitting, right? The stretchy kind. I'll have to be thorough."

"No, don't touch me. I'm helpless when you touch me. I told you…"

He grabbed her as she tried to slip past him. "What? That you have to love me? No sex unless we're in love. Well, I'm in love."

Dinah melted the moment his arms stopped their sparking. "No, of course I don't love you," she sputtered. "I hardly know you."

He kissed her mouth as though starved for it and she responded. The next thing she knew they had fallen to the clothing covered bed. Dinah shoved the items aside as he pushed her back against the pillows. She wanted the moment to never end. But yet, she did. Confusion reigned in her heart. *How could she concede so easily?*

"Your breasts," he said. "I may have to measure them more than once to get it just right." He kissed her neck and ran his hands through her hair, pulling her closer and beneath him.

She sighed deeply as his hands slipped under her flimsy T-shirt and caressed her lightly. And her breath caught in her throat as one of his hands strayed lower, across her abdomen, then down to her thighs. She closed her eyes savoring the thrill that grew with each new area of exploration. She clasped him tighter, wanting to feel the whole length of his body pressed against hers. She was clearly losing the battle with herself.

"Dinah, open your eyes," Nero said in a voice that had suddenly lost its husky tone.

"What?" She did as he instructed, then burst out laughing. They were somewhere near the ceiling. "Well," she said with what she hoped passed for dignity. "It's a good thing we're over a bed since you don't think much of my landing technique."

A knock on the door prevented any further conversation.

"Maid service!" A foreign voice hailed from the door, as the key turned in the lock.

In her haste to get them down, Dinah

dropped them too near the edge of the bed and they both tumbled onto the floor just as the door opened.

"Oh! Sorry, miss," came the maid's plaintive response as she backed out and slammed the door.

Nero leaned back against the side of the bed with a huge smile. "I give up, no sex. Maybe we ought to dye my hair and get ready for Rafael."

Dinah stood. "Saved by the cleaning crew. Some fortitude I have." She blew him a kiss. "I'll shower, you can dye your hair in the sink. I see he brought the comb-through kind, not very permanent, but it's a start." She rubbed his chin. "I saw a razor on the sink." She gathered her new clothes, held them at arm's length, and said, "Ugh, I am going to look sooo... dumpy in this."

~*~

Nero stood facing her when she exited the

bathroom. He said nothing but she could see something had changed.

"What now? She asked. "What's happened? You have the countenance of a zombie."

He let out a long breath as though he had been holding it for ages. "First of all, when I squeezed the tube of shaving cream, it shot across the room. The muscle bunching I talked about, struck again. Nero the powerful is more than a name definition it seems."

"Great, so you can 'reach' and you have super strength. Why so glum?"

"I'm not glum, merely a little startled at the moment. So, then I shaved and I cut myself."

"Oh, you poor baby." Dinah peered at his face. "I don't see any cuts. It must not have been too bad."

"You don't see any cuts because the blood became a pink smoke and disappeared, as did the cut."

"Wow! I hope I have that power. That's bloody amazing." She grinned, "Little pun there."

"Very little." But he smiled, too. "Rafe is going to flip out, and he should be back soon.

Dinah heard the door open. "Speaking of Rafe."

"You were followed," Nero said, his posture suddenly rigid.

"No, I'm pretty sure I wasn't."

"Trust me, you were. They're still a few miles away, but they are on their way. They're looking at a device mounted on the dashboard, they must have planted something on your car. Hurry, we have to find it. Grab the packs and head out. We'll each take a section of the car; they had to plant it on the run so it shouldn't be hard to find.

In less than a minute Nero found it on the rear bumper and put it in his pocket.

"Will you dispose of it or do you want me to?" Rafael asked.

"I will, but not here. Drive to the nearest mall, we can attach it to a car like yours. They'll think you went inside and it will give us some time before they figure out we have it. You have a screwdriver in this car? If possible, we'll switch the plates."

~*~

It took a while, but they were able to make the switch with little or no trouble. Once they were on the interstate headed north, Rafael retrieved an envelope from his jacket pocket and passed it over the back seat to Dinah. "From the professor. I dropped your chain and coin in it. We never spoke, by the way. The minute I touched the coin, he just handed me the envelope and left. He did it so deftly I thought no one saw him, but I guess they were focused like hawks. Your letter is there, too, I never got a chance to give it to him."

Dinah opened the envelope from Dumas, read the first page and frowned. "Wait, we have to go back, right away."

Rafe eyed her in the rearview mirror. "We're ten miles down the road, Dinah."

"I know, but it's the key to a safety deposit box; he had me sign on to it years ago, in case something happened to him. The note says it's urgent I open it now. It says it will answer all my questions."

"We'll get a rent-a-car and Dinah and I can go back and meet you later," Nero offered.

"No," Dinah insisted. "I'll take a taxi, no matter what it costs. A rental car requires a credit card. They're sure to be watching for one of us to use one. And I'll go alone; they won't be looking for me as a redhead."

Nero sat up front with Rafael. He turned to face her. "I'm afraid something will happen to you. I'll go with you."

"I can fly away if I have to, can you?"

"No, but I can tell you when danger approaches."

"Nero's right. You both go." Rafael handed Nero a cell phone. "Here's another throw away. Call me when you are safely out of town again and I'll come and get you. I plugged in my new cell number. I'll work on a plan and find a place for us to hide out. Our big problem is going to be money. Take a bag or two into the bank with you in case the old boy left you a bundle."

"I doubt he's rich, at least he doesn't live extravagantly, but I did often wonder why he lived so simply. He once spoke of foreign investments he had." She shrugged. "You may have a point—maybe he's been stashing money away." She watched the signs indicating an exit that had more than a motel and a gas station. "The sooner we get off, the sooner we get back." She pointed. "Take the next exit ramp. It's not a huge town but they're bound to have hungry taxi drivers."

Nero tossed his bag over the seat next to Dinah's. "Let's leave our backpacks and just take our wallets and the expandable tote bags. We'll be less conspicuous that way."

CHAPTER FIVE

Dinah walked a few steps behind Nero, letting her eyes scan the area in front of and alongside them, but he was the lead dog with the talent for sensing trouble by 'reaching.' The building they sought sat at the end of the street in an older section of town, one referred to as the historic section. Historic, she thought, if your idea of historic meant 60 years ago, more or less. Still, the street had personality, with the three-story row-houses lining either side, all of which had been recently converted to offices and specialty shops. Tiny tables shaded by brightly colored umbrellas dotted the area next to one called *Contesa's Tea Room*. They had gone so far as to use faux cobblestones to replace the sidewalks and the lamps edging the curb resembled gas lights from another era.

Nero glanced back at her. "I thought you said it was a safety deposit box. I assumed that meant a bank. The place looks like a prison."

"Yes, it doesn't exactly fit the landscape, does it? It actually was a small prison at one time, before the town expanded and surrounded it. I imagine the guards and other staff lived in the row-houses once. Anyway, the sturdy construction made it easy to convert the building into a private, and rather exclusive, repository. All they lock up now is other peoples' valuables."

They mounted the steps to the revolving doors that provided entry. "And here we are." She announced with wave of one arm.

In spite of their ludicrous outfits, and because she had identification and a key, accessing the private chamber and retrieving the box required little time. Even maids and house painters could salt away valuables.

Once alone, they sat together at the table provided while she inserted the key. The box was larger than she expected, but then she had no idea what it might contain. Dinah gently raised the lid. She heard Nero gasp.

An impressive pile of coins, similar to the one she wore around her neck glittered in the bottom of the box. Next to it were several large envelopes and a thick notebook. She snuck a peek into one of the envelopes. It contained a great deal of paper money and several account books on foreign banks. "Oh, my God! I had no idea what we would find, and I'm not entirely sure I grasp the whole of it yet."

Nero shook his head. "I know you said you didn't know what the coins were, were you serious?"

"As serious as a goofball can be," she said with a smile. "Well, the note said to empty the box, which doesn't mean the contents are mine. Perhaps he believes the authorities will try to confiscate it and he wants me to move it for safekeeping."

Nero smiled. "Dinah, look around you. This *is* safekeeping? But I guess 'they' could get a warrant to search anything nowadays. I suggest we take everything as he requested and read all the paperwork once we get somewhere away from prying eyes. In other words, let's get out of here," he added. "Our out-of-town taxi driver may attract attention."

"He's in the underground garage, but you're right." They bundled everything into the tote bags they'd brought for the purpose and hurried out the door.

The property Rafe had procured for them reminded Dinah more of a fish camp than it did a house, but its remote location and ramshackle appearance belied its true charm. She found the inside decorated with fishnets and seashells, making it feel touristy, but homey. There were three small bedrooms tacked on as afterthoughts, much like Nero's bathroom. A bubbling stream ran along one side of the house and a small playground graced the other. It contained swings and a see-saw, both were rusty and the swings squeaked when Dinah gave them a push. Their presence suggested a family had once lived there.

Rafe made light of the acquisition. "It belongs to a friend of a friend's relative. It's been sold to developers, but the owner can't get here for several months to clear out his personal belongings. We're the current caretakers. And don't worry about price. He just doesn't want the locals cleaning it out before he can. The developers don't take possession until the first of the year." He walked over to the far bedroom door. "I'm going to put a few hours in on the book, then take a nap, so we'll discuss a plan later."

As soon as his door closed, Dinah emptied the

tote bags onto the table and sorted out the contents. "Nero, look at all this money! There's a small fortune here." She noticed his frown.

"Do you suppose it's all legal? Didn't you say he was a professor? I thought they worked for the joy of dispensing knowledge. He must have been moonlighting."

"Stop it! Don't make insinuations. He's a wonderful, kind and gentle man who wouldn't steal a candy bar. Maybe he inherited money and invested it, or just invested his savings wisely. And don't forget, he worked as a scientist long before he was a professor. I told you he is brilliant. Now sit down and help me count the money."

Nero sighed. "Okay, okay. It just seems odd, that's all. I'm more interested in what he has to say in those letters and the journal than I am in how much he stashed away over the years."

"First we count; then we read. We can't live on Rafael's generosity. New identities will cost money, plus we have to eat and find a place to live."

"What, no ice cave or bat mobile in our future?"

"Count!" She said.

The actual total came to nearly $90,000, and the overseas accounts held millions. Dinah sat back in her chair as they made the final tally, then rose and went to the kitchen area. "I believe wine is called for," she proclaimed as she fetched a cold bottle of Chardonnay from the refrigerator."

"It seems your friend raised thrift to an art form."

Dinah poured two glasses and set them on the table. "Let's not be judgmental until we've read the documents." She tossed him one of the manila envelopes full of papers. "There will be no secrets, okay?"

He nodded, and selected the first pages to study.

She picked up the one with her name emblazoned across the front and started to read.

My Dearest Dinah,

If you have opened this missive, I am no doubt among the missing. I have so much to tell you I'm not certain where to begin. Unfortunately, I must start by frightening you. I am an alien. Where from, matters not, but alien I am. My ancestors migrated from a distant solar system before your world evolved. Since one truth leads quite naturally to another, you are also alien, although only half....

Dinah went rigid. She dropped the papers on the table, unable to concentrate after absorbing the shock of the first few sentences.

Nero looked up from the papers in front of him. "Good grief! What's wrong, you look as though the world just ended."

Dinah reached over and took the papers from him. "It seems I do have secrets," she said. A tear ran down her cheek and she trembled.

Nero came and stood behind her. "Whatever it is, we can fix it. We're a team now, remember. You only read a few words, what could he have said to inspire such a reaction? Is it a suicide note?"

She folded the paper over so he couldn't see it. "No, it isn't. It's...maybe he's senile, or crazy and I didn't recognize the signs. I need to read more."

"Please don't shut me out, whatever it is I'll help you."

Dinah now faced the ultimate test. Although she constantly insisted she didn't 'know' Nero, she had never felt closer to anyone in her life. In a matter of days all her realities had dissolved into fragments, fraught with new obstacles at every turn, not the least of which was her raging attraction to Nero. *But how do you trust someone with information like this?* You throw caution to the proverbial wind, she decided. She pulled out a chair for him.

"You may want to be seated to read this."

Nero squeezed her shoulder, setting off sparks; then did as she suggested. "Okay, you super-hero woman, let me have it." He read the first words without speaking, although he did turn pale.

When he continued to read, Dinah bit down on her lower lip. When he finally turned over the third page she could stand it no longer. "Come on, show some reaction."

"You didn't read far enough, apparently. According to the professor, half the inhabitants of Earth are aliens, or, are descended from them."

"What? Let me see that." She snatched the pages from him and began to read. She picked up where she had left off.

...only half. You mother was an Earthling. And I don't mean the woman you perceive to be your mother, I'm referring to your birth mother, Nadine. And yes, I am your father. Although it was forbidden for me to associate romantically with her, it just happened. I loved her dearly. When we learned she was pregnant, she left so the tzars wouldn't find out, otherwise they would have taken you and your twin brother away the minute you were born. Children of such unions are sometimes

born with limitless power, and are greatly feared.

Thousands of years ago when we first came to this solar system, our resemblance to humans was so exact, we saw no reason not to mingle. We had no idea what would happen to offspring of the two species. We didn't have super powers and neither did Earthlings. We found out the hard way. Giants and geniuses were the result, and not all those born with power proved beneficent, so the practice was outlawed. A genetic artifact continued for some time, but wore off after several generations. The only true remnant of those unions was a recessive gene on chromosome 16. It causes a mutation in the MC1R protein which produces red hair. That redhead mutation is now reflected in 2% of the world's population. But the mutation bestows no special powers. It does make those who carry the gene, all redheads, harder to sedate, often requiring

20% more anesthesia, at the same time making them more sensitive to pain. Among some Polynesian tribes red haired people are revered and are believed to be descended from gods. Well, we descended from somewhere else, but we are certainly not gods.

"I'm sure you have questions about your brother, Max, and I regret I cannot divulge wonderful things to excite you. Unfortunately, he represents the reason we do not mate with humans. Even as a toddler, he was a sterling example of what can go wrong. I do not know how much power Max has, or, if like you, he has none at all, because I lost track of him at an early age. I only know he will never use whatever talent he has except to further himself. In a word, he is, evil. We separated you as babes after he tried to suffocate you while you slept. I'm sorry. It's fair to say that when good and evil were proportioned, the gods chose to divide

them evenly in this case.

~*~

Nero smiled as she looked up. "See, you aren't the only one, but you are special."

Dinah clenched her fists. "But I'm an alien with an evil twin, don't you see? And my whole life is a lie. The professor is my father. No wonder I felt so drawn to him. I don't fault him for any of this, but...am I really an alien? And where is my dreadful twin brother?"

"I can't answer about your brother, but if you are an alien, you're a sexy alien."

"Oh how I love your one track mind, but could you *please* stop the silliness for just one minute and help me figure things out!"

"Sorry, I wanted to make light of it. Look, I don't care what you are, it doesn't change how I feel about you. And an hour ago you were thrilled at the idea of being a superhero; how is this so different?"

"I'm befuddled, and I can't unscramble

my brain. Until I went near the pool, I was as normal as any human. Something there triggered it, probably that blasted cloud." She sighed. "We need to read all of this stuff," she indicated the envelopes and the journal.

After they hid the money, which the letter divulged now belonged to her, they used the rest of the afternoon to read the contents of the envelopes. They saved the journal for later since it revealed the professors personal observations on life in general. Because they now knew he was her father as well as her friend, Nero suggested she read it alone, and share only what she chose.

According to Dumas, the weather phenomena were also beings, he called them *guardians*, and they were from the home planet. They stand guard over the portal to the lower world, where others like the professor reside. Unlike the professor, the guardians have no structure other than pure energy, and their sole purpose is to prepare those entering the depths for the journey. Because the guardians recognized Dinah's DNA, they struck, preparing her for entrance to their world by way of the pool. The whirlpool would have taken her there had Nero not pulled her from the water at the last minute.

"Now I understand why he never wanted me to go near the mountain. He knew the guardians of the portal would recognize me as one of their own. Did my brother go there? Did the pool give him hidden talents? Where is he? If Max found the pool, maybe they took him to the…underworld, or whatever it's called." Dinah shivered at the thought.

Something bothered her, tickled at the back of her mind, something to do with Nero. "The energy from the guardians must have ignited my dormant super powers, but why did you get them? Maybe you're part alien, too."

"That very thought occurred to me. It might be because we were, ah…joined at the moment it struck, and some of it rubbed off on me, as it were. As for your brother, I suggest we leave that dilemma for future deliberation. We have enough to deal with in the present. There will come a time to address his disappearance."

"Okay, I can live with both ideas, for now."

"I'm fascinated by this *lower world* revelation. What's it like, how many people live there, and how many more of them are up here, like the professor?" Nero picked up the nearest pile of papers. "How much of this do we tell Rafael?"

Dinah put her elbows on the table and her chin on her palms. "Everything, he has to know it all if he is going to be part of this. We'll just let him read the same things we did. I just wish we could talk to the professor. I have a thousand questions. But since that's out, why don't you tell me about Rafael, what's his story? The name sounds Spanish, but he doesn't have an accent and he doesn't look Spanish either."

"Ah, yes, the mysterious Rafe. He does

have an odd background, which makes him fit
perfectly in our company. Some Key West
fishermen found him when he was a child,
unconscious, and laying on top of an overturned
sailboat. He was alone and no one knows how
long he'd been floating there. He was seriously
sunburned and dehydrated. The fishermen, being
devout Catholics, brought him to the sisters at the
local convent. When he regained consciousness,
he would repeat over and over…and they're the
only words he would say: 'My name is Rafael
Zapata, I am four years old.' Assuming he was a
Cuban refugee, several Cuban families offered to
adopt him, but he would have nothing to do with
them. Although the sisters did their best, other
than his first statement, he didn't speak for
almost a year. Then one day a young couple
came to enroll their daughter in the parochial
school. As they passed Rafe, who sat on a bench
outside the mother superior's office, they spoke
quietly to each other. Rafe heard them. He
suddenly sprang from his seat and latched onto
the woman, screaming and crying at the same

time. They couldn't pry him away. And he spoke for the first time–in French."

"In French?"

"Yes, the couple was French, and that's the history of our mysterious Rafe, in its entirety. To this day he has no clue as to how he got there or who he is. After all, at four years old…and by then a year had passed. I know the circumstances of his origin trouble him deeply at times. He often broods and I wonder if that's what made him become a writer. Now for the happy ending, the couple adopted him and he loves them. He and their daughter remain very close."

"But there is still something missing for him." Dinah ventured, understanding. "I always knew there was something odd about my family, perhaps I sensed I wasn't theirs. I know I often felt like an outsider at home. Them keeping the secret from me may be part of it. It was them and me, never 'us.'" She pushed the envelopes aside. "Enough of my whining, tonight we act. As soon as it gets dark, why don't we fly to see your tailor?"

He stacked the envelopes and put them back in one of the tote bags. "And Rafe can use the time to catch up on what we've read. And now that we have lots of money, he can find us a permanent place of our own. He set up the website earlier today. The border on the opening page is made of toddlers holding hands. He says it's secure and he'll tweak it once a week to keep it that way. He also has it set up to alert us with news items on children."

~*~

Rafael accepted the alien news better than expected; in fact he thought it rather exciting. "Hey, I write science fiction, remember? Oh, by the way, I did pick up a news item that might interest you. There's a missing child, he strayed from a summer camp for children with disabilities, a nine-year-old named, Harry Stanbeck. They believe him to have simply wandered off, but they can't be sure. The problem is, he's deaf." He handed them a printout of the map he'd downloaded off the webcast. "Since it will be dark soon, you may want to do a search of your own before you head for Mr. Lau's. A small search party plans to work through the night, so be careful to avoid them."

Nero studied the printout. "Well, we can't call out to him in any case, so what did you have in mind? I know Dinah has enhanced vision, she can see for miles; that might help."

Rafe nodded. "Hmm…I was wondering if maybe your innate sense of danger might pick up on the boy. So far, you've only sensed danger to yourselves, but you may find the ability works for others. There's nothing to lose by trying." Rafe handed them some calling cards. "I made them for you to hand out. I used Dinah's sketches of you both in costume. If you truly plan to be heroic, you need to build a reputation, and the cards will lead people to our Internet site."

~*~

The moonless night helped cover their flight

path. The area they had to cover was almost thirty miles due west and Dinah chose to go slowly for their first evening event.

Once in the area, Nero leaned near Dinah's ear. I *reached* and I feel something. I see through the eyes of several people, they're all very tense and focused. One of them is picturing the boy, he must know him. He's crying, and I feel sure he is the father of the boy."

Dinah narrowed her eyes and swept the area for miles on either side of them as they cruised above the treetops. "I see red glowing blotches I believe are, deer, bears and people, and all kinds of things, they're all over the place. The forest is filled with creatures. It must be their life energy I'm seeing. It's amazing and it's scary."

Nero tightened his grip on Dinah. "Something unusual keeps calling to me, but when I *reach* I can't understand what I'm seeing. This person sees differently."

"Harry is deaf, perhaps he sees differently, maybe in symbols or signs. It could be him."

"Maybe. Or it could be that children in general see differently. Go another mile and a little to your right."

When they neared the area he indicated, he tapped her shoulder. "Yes, I feel the danger he senses and his fear; I think we're close."

"I see a smaller heat blur just ahead; it's either a small animal or a child. I'm going to try to land a little away from him so as not to frighten him further."

"Try not to frighten me, too, okay? Landing upright would be an improvement."

"No backseat flying allowed. Brace yourself."

They landed in some prickly bushes, but it helped soften their landing. A bed of pine needles kept the vegetation to a minimum on the forest floor and allowed them to walk freely beneath the pines. Nero used the small flashlight he had brought along, fanning it back and forth to attract the boy's attention and draw him out. He was rewarded with the sound of running footsteps.

"Dinah, I'm getting those muscle bunching spasms again, whatever that means."

"It means—don't squeeze anything!"

Suddenly the boy appeared between the trees in front of them.

Dinah stepped forward and drew him into her arms. "It's okay, it's okay," she said soothingly, even though she knew he didn't hear her. Instincts rule, she thought.

Nero put his hand on the boys shoulder to add to his comfort. The boy collapsed the instant he touched him. Nero jumped back.

"Did you squeeze his shoulder? I told you not to squeeze anything. What happened?" Dinah dropped to her knees beside the boy.

"No, no. I didn't! I merely placed my hand on his shoulder lightly. Maybe he's gone into shock."

Dinah picked the child up. "I'm going to fly him to the edge of the campground where someone will find him quickly. He may have other medical problems we don't know about. Wait here, I won't be long. Lend me your flashlight. If I shine it in someone's face they won't be able to see me."

"Be careful."

As she flew, she recalled Nero saying one man might be his father. She had carefully noted the man's bright aura when she realized each person's glow was as telling as fingerprints, no two were the same. She looked for his aura now as she moved over the landscape. She would have to risk having him see her fly.

It only required a minute for her to spot him, and he remained separate from the others. She came in as slowly as she dared, concentrating on making this landing perfect. She alit in an upright position, directly in his path.

The man stood open mouthed for a second; then bellowed, "Harry, my God, you found him. How did you do it?"

Dinah handed Harry to him and placed one finger to her lips. The flashlight idea had failed without a free hand to use it. "Tell no one, promise."

Just then Harry woke up. It appeared he

was traumatized. He wrapped his arms over his head and buried it in his father's shoulder.

Dinah slowly rose into the air as the father watched. She hoped he wouldn't faint like his son had.

She found Nero sitting with his back against a tree. He motioned for her to sit beside him. "The search party will clear out now, so let's rest for a minute."

"I brought the boy to the man you identified as his father."

Nero reached out and pulled Dinah to him. Once the sparks receded, he kissed her gently, then long and hard, till they were both breathless. "We should wait at least a half hour for the searchers to disperse. Have you ever made love on a forest floor?" he asked softly, as he unbuttoned her blouse and trailed his finger down from her neckline.

Dinah wasn't about to tell him she had never made love anywhere, to anyone. If she ever did, if she had to choose a lover, Nero would be the one, but she wanted more than a quick love affair. The temperate affection she had suffered as a child she suspected was the result of her parent's unhappy marriage. She wanted more and she had to get it right the first time.

Nero pressed her. "Why won't you let me make love to you? Has someone wounded you before, are you afraid to fall in love? You said yourself, we're a team now. Why not become lovers?"

She pulled away from him. "I've never been in love, I'm not sure if I'd know the difference between love and lust. We've known each other less than a week."

Nero looked incredulous. "What? You've never ever been in love? Not even puppy love? He sat up straighter. "Wait a minute, are you telling me what I think you are?"

Dinah sprang to her feet. "I'm not telling you anything." She looked down at her blouse which had somehow come untucked again. Every time he came near she ended up half naked. *What the heck was wrong with her*? Nero's touch made her lose control like a giddy teenager. "Come on, we need to get to that tailor before the sun comes up."

"It's not even midnight," he said with a laugh. "And you're avoiding my questions. But that's okay because I believe I've guessed the answer."

"You haven't guessed anything. Change the subject! Let's go see that tailor of yours. Mr. Lau is it? We have important things to do, and it's time to stop this silly romance stuff! I don't love you, okay? And I'll tell you why, since it's so important to you. Because I really don't know you!"

Nero grinned at her. "It doesn't feel very silly to me. I'm nuts about you."

Dinah was livid. He had only known her for a few days and he could play her like a musical instrument, pulling her strings to a rhythm she felt down to her toes. She was learning fast. Sex was a symphony and Nero was a maestro.

~*~

Mr. Lau was quiet and polite to a fault. He constantly bowed and maintained a truly unreadable expression. The word inscrutable came to mind, causing her to smile. But whatever he was thinking was not relevant because he worked with such speed and precision that she was awed. As soon as she gave him her drawings, he went right to work. She considered telling Nero to remind Lau that their mission was secret, but didn't since she knew this gentle man would be insulted by such instruction. Trust, like friendship is often recognized in an instant. *Was love, too?* She dared not go there.

CHAPTER SIX

Dinah rose early the next morning and found Rafael already up and making breakfast. His dark sleek hair was pulled back in a ponytail as he worked his magic at the stove. He was definitely movie star material. She wondered if he had a girlfriend. She would ask Nero.

"You made headlines this morning. I would love to get my hands on the supermarket rags, they could run for weeks on what the boy told them last night."

Dinah bunched her shoulders. "Oh, oh! Tell me the worst. I guess we should have waited to be costumed before we activated our roles. I honestly didn't think the father could see me very well."

"Oh, the father denied seeing you at all. It's the boy who has the tabloids humming. According to him, a flaming red-haired angel swept him into her arms and flew him to safety. He did say he dreamed it, which works for me. Do you actually glow in the dark, by the way?" Rafael removed a pancake from the frying pan and poured in more batter.

"I doubt it, I'll have to ask Nero," she said, and then realized how that sounded when she saw Rafael's eyebrows raise. "I mean he was there with me in the dark, you know?"

"Right." He winked at her.

"Pfft! Anyway, what did the father say happened?" She had asked him to say nothing, but under the circumstances would certainly forgive him if he'd ignored her plea.

"He said he found the boy asleep, leaning against the base of a tree, and when he took him in his arms, the boy awoke and told him, through sign language, about the angel in his dreams. Alas, the story doesn't end there. Apparently the boy saw your Internet card on his father's nightstand and correctly guessed the picture to be of you. But the real shocker will curl you already curly hair."

"Ouch! Do not play games with me, Rafe. What is it?"

Rafael turned from the stove and faced her. "The boy can hear perfectly now."

Dinah shrieked. "That's...that's unreal. It must have been Nero's touch. Remember? He healed his own face when he cut it shaving? He must have healing powers that extend to others, as well. He said a few moments before he touched the boy that he felt his muscles bunching again. It means something. Every time he gets that feeling something bizarre happens." She didn't mention what happened whenever he touched her. *Could that be it? Had he absorbed some power from the pool that drew her to his touch?* It was too much to consider before breakfast. And it would mean it wasn't love.

Subconsciously, she realized, she wanted it to be love.

"The emails have been pouring in," he continued. "Fan mail mostly. I have to find a way to manage it so we don't miss something important. I didn't see any cries for help yet, but this could prove time-consuming."

She nodded and glanced at the stove meaningfully. "I can see that. Ah...do I get one of those?"

"Sure." He slid the next pancake onto a heated plate and handed it to her. "How long before you get the costumes?"

"Tomorrow night."

"I have some news, too." He smiled. "I've arranged the purchase of a small island. It will make the perfect hideout. It's in the Florida Keys, a very private Key of our very own, accessed by a one-way bridge that we can easily secure. It has a very old, very large mansion on it, along with eight cabins scattered along the opposite shore from the main building. My thought was that in case we ever needed to harbor someone for protection, the cabins would serve us well."

"How do we manage so much property by ourselves? It sounds as though we will need staff."

"I'm working on the staffing. Why not recruit Nero's Vietnamese tailor. Nero once told me that Mr. Lau has a talent for more than alterations. He's also a consummate gardener. Perhaps we can interest him in a position as grounds keeper. I understand he's a recluse; he might consider relocating if he has no personal ties to his neighbors."

"Yes! He's a lovely man, so quiet and unassuming. We can start with him, but we will need others."

"And we'll find them. It also occurs to me Mr. Lau may have relatives we could import, ones who speak little or no English, which would also be advantageous. He's currently a poor man without resources and a confirmed loner, just the type to fit into our scenario and we'd get help him at the same time. Broach the subject when you pick up the costumes."

"You're a genius. What would we do without you?"

Rafael grinned and used his forearm to reposition a dark lock of hair that had escaped his ponytail and fallen across his forehead. "Probably pretty well, but I'm loving this. I haven't had this much fun in years. My life has new meaning, I feel useful and stimulated. Quite honestly, like most fiction writers, I find the real world dull at times, which is probably the reason behind my unquenchable drive to pen escapist novels. Flying superheroes who heal? Come on! Nothing I could create on the written page compares to the excitement of being involved in the real deal with the pair of you."

Dinah laughed. "You think?"

"As a writer though, I have to tell you, I'm equally curious about your evil twin. Where is he and what is he up to? Does he possess the same abilities? And most importantly, why did he try to kill you as a child? His role in my script would be a very active one. What I'm hinting at here is that once he knows where you are, he may come after you again. You need to be on guard, I perceive him as your nemesis."

Dinah cringed. "And to think, I always longed for a sibling."

Nero emerged from the back bedroom. He quickly joined them with a tense smile. "I sense something, what they refer to in horror movies as impending doom. I'm registering a huge case of it.

Rafael's cell phone beeped softly as though in response to Nero's announcement.

Rafael looked at the dial and flipped the phone open "Yes, Kurt?" He listened quietly for a moment, then snapped his fingers and pointed to the television.

Dinah grabbed the remote and turned it on. Either the owner of the cabin hadn't paid the bill or someone had shut it down. The screen displayed pure static.

"Thanks, Kurt. I think I may leave under the circumstances, you know how I value my privacy when I'm working." He dropped the phone on the table. "Kurt owns the property.

Apparently you were seen flying last night, well, not you exactly. Several people reported seeing 'something' in the evening sky. For now they're calling it a UFO, a rather handy cover story for us. In the meantime, several conspicuous cars, carrying men in dark suits, have been combing the countryside this morning, asking questions about new people in the area."

Dinah continued to play with the television remote; she even tried the radio, to no avail.

Rafael rapped the front of the TV screen and threw his hands in the air. "They're government, who else can jam the media. Our cell phones will be next. Time to move on I'm afraid. I had hoped we would have more time, but...."

"Right," Nero agreed. He cautioned Dinah. "I think we should hike out through the wilderness and let Rafael drive out of here alone. Let's get packing. I keep *reaching*, but they're still too far away for me to know if they're headed here. We don't want to get surrounded."

Dinah prepared for action. "You pack for both of us and I'll clean up the kitchen and neaten up so it doesn't look as though anyone was here."

"Forget cleaning up, we've left fingerprints everywhere, you'd never get them all. And it no longer matters, they know who we are. It's time for us to become other people." Nero looked at Rafael. "If you go now, you might get clear before they close in."

"Rafael," Dinah said. "Give me the map of the Keys and all your paperwork, in case they stop you. We'll meet you on the island in a few days."

Five minutes later, Dinah and Nero had donned their heavy backpacks and slipped out the back door of the cabin and locked it behind them. They followed the shoreline for a mile or so before heading into the dense forest. A soft breeze picked up, bringing with it the promise of an early fall. Dinah would miss the changing of the leaves, but the subtropical climate of the Keys would soon bury her regrets. She hoped. She had spent her life exploring the great northwest. Things evolve, she decided and she would evolve with them.

The unmistakable roar of heavy vehicles in the distance chilled her. "Do you suppose they've captured Rafael?"

"I hope not," Nero frowned. "They have no real reason to detain him, however, I doubt reason will determine how they operate from now on. It's you and me they want, and they probably realize he's key to finding us. I'm glad he gave you all his paperwork on the property." He stopped and faced her. "Rafe won't tell them anything."

"But they have ways…drugs to make him talk." Dinah clenched her fists in frustration.

"We don't know they have him. Let's not jump to conclusions."

CHAPTER SEVEN

Miles away, Colonel Jake Preston spoke with four of his best men. They'd convened at a long abandoned gas station on the outskirts of a small private hunting preserve, marked by no-trespassing signs every quarter mile or so.

"The federal agents said there were some new people staying up by this lake," Jake said, pointing to a spot on the map, then inched his finger to the top of the page. "I want the four of you stationed on the far side of these woods. Judging by what the agents said about their quick action up at the pool, I have a feeling our missing trekkers are going to know we're coming and make a run for it again."

He looked around at the rest of his crew, pleased with what he saw. They were an elite group, the very best black ops the military had to offer and they were his personal best. "The pentagon has a priority interest in these two, and the order was to apprehend them pronto. Tranquilizer darts only, I don't care if they shoot at you with Uzis, bring them in unharmed."

They grunted a few, 'yes sirs', and nodded in unison.

"Remember, unofficially this is a training exercise. Officially, this may well be one of the most important assignments you will ever have. Treat   it   that   way.

"Sir?" One of the young NCO's asked. "May I ask just who these people are? Isn't one of them a woman? Are they terrorists?"

"All right, Sergeant, if you really must know, and since you all have clearance and you're sworn to secrecy, I'm going to tell you.

They're not people, and they're not terrorists, they're aliens!"

The officer's mouth dropped open. "Aliens, sir? But they look like regular people, right?"

"You ever seen a regular person fly, son?"

"No, sir."

"Exactly. And now that I have your full attention. Do your job."

A soldier jumped from a slow moving Humvee and ran over to the Colonel. "They have the road block in place, sir, and they've detained a man in a car similar to the one you're looking for."

"Is he alone? And is he the man we have photos of?"

"Yes to the first question and no to the second. He looks slightly foreign, says his name is Zapata."

"Let him go. Apologize for detaining him and explain it's an exercise. We don't want to stir up the locals any more than the feds already have."

Jake watched the man run back to his vehicle and thought about the road block. Damn civilians were going to be a problem on this mission, and this mission was a career maker for him. He acted on direct orders from the president himself. He was scheduled to report to him in person tomorrow morning.

Aliens. He still couldn't believe it himself. This really was the mission of a lifetime and he planned to capitalize on it. One small misstep would mean the end, so he couldn't afford to miss a trick or he'd be standing guard duty on some bum-fuck forgotten post. In fact, he knew men who had been eliminated for lesser failures. It occurred to him only momentarily that with a name like Zapata, the civilian could be an illegal, but he dismissed the notion, it was too far north. Besides, the difference between illegal aliens and aliens with a capital A, was light years apart, literally. Jake laughed aloud at his little joke.

He turned back to his men. "Time to

show those G-men how it's done. Don't just stand there, bring me those frigging aliens!"

CHAPTER EIGHT

The thick soft floor of the forest eased their forward momentum. The silence sharpened Dinah's already heightened senses, letting her discern the different calls of birds and the rustle of deer hundreds of feet before she saw them. And when she narrowed her eyes and focused, she detected the slightest movement in the deepest shadows, but it was Nero's fine-tuning for danger she counted on.

"There are four of them," Nero said. "And they're scared of us. Why would they be?"

"Think about it, Nero. A week ago if I

saw someone fly, I'd be afraid of what else they might be able to do. In any case, I think I heard a helicopter a few minutes ago, which makes flying a risky solution, but I'm willing to try if you like. However, the very idea of having a helicopter chase us through the morning sky does not thrill me."

"Exactly, so we fly only as a last resort. If we knew what speeds you were capable of it might be an option." He came to an abrupt halt. "Someone looked at me, from above the ground, I don't understand his position. Can he fly, too?"

"The trees," Dinah cautioned, grasping the extent of their error. "We've been looking out, not up. Think sniper."

"Ouch!" Nero cried out, seconds before he hit the ground.

Dinah dropped beside him, certain he'd been shot. *Please don't let him be dead, she prayed silently.* She felt for a pulse, but heard nothing but the thundering of her own. She saw no blood, but the look on his face frightened her. She had seen death before, at her cousins' funerals. They had looked peaceful, Nero did not; he looked conflicted. Death had too many faces, and she didn't have the desire to interpret them.

Without warning, a fury, unmatched by anything she'd ever experienced came over her, like a fast festering fever. She peered into Nero's blank face again. His eyes were open and she saw no movement of his chest to indicate he still breathed. That's when she spied the tiny dart embedded in his neck below his left ear. She tore it out. An ache fought for purchase in her soul, but the rising anger won out. She gave in to it with an all-consuming gusto.

Rising slowly into the air, Dinah sought a target. Her eyes did a quick scan of the tree tops for a mile in all directions and she mentally filed the location of all four men. They were a good distance away, but she could clearly see the fear radiating from their eyes when they glimpsed her suspended in air. Dinah drew in a deep breath and a surge of power propelled her to within feet of the first one. She hovered before him; then raised one arm and clenched her fist. A spear of blue sparks struck him and he dropped to the forest floor like a rock. Whirling she charged to her next attacker. She continued until she had stunned them all into unconsciousness. The entire assault took place in a nano-second.

The next thing she knew she was flying faster than a freight train, with Nero in her arms. Tears ran down her cheeks only to be dried instantly by the force of the headwind.

After ten minutes or so, Dinah slowed and examined the landscape. Ahead of her a lonely mountain meadow beckoned. She felt faint from the adrenaline rush of the past half hour. Her senses demanded rest. She landed gently as a feather, wishing Nero could see it and congratulate her for finally getting it right.

She laid him on a carpet of wild flowers and stretched out beside him. She draped one arm across his chest, wishing for the usual sparks at contact but saw only one small flash, like the final moments of a light bulb as it burns out. He remained dead.

Dinah wept herself to exhaustion, finally

falling asleep with her head on Nero's shoulder.

In her dream, he spoke to her. "I told you I love you," he whispered against her ear. "This healing business presents more challenges than I anticipated. I could hear your every word and see your torrent of tears but whatever they used on the dart, paralyzed me, leaving me incapable of responding."

Dinah shot to a sitting position. It wasn't a dream, Nero lived.

"I recall a dreamy state," he continued, "which I can only describe as hibernation, because my body shut down to deal with the effects of the drug. I know you thought I was dead, but there was no way for me to reassure you."

"Nero, Nero, Nero! I wanted to die, too." She threw her arms around him, relieved for the first time to see sparks, a million happy sparks, she thought. She kissed them away. "So many thoughts went through my head. Going on without you wasn't a possibility."

Nero smothered her conversation with his

mouth. "Have I not told you I love you, goof-ball? Well, I do. I never knew I could feel like this with anyone." He raised a hand against her protest. "Don't say it has to do with the pool and what happened. I confess, I knew before. The minute I saw you at the trekking sign-in, something in my heart told me you were the one. I fought it at first by acting like a chauvinist and a boor, but I knew."

Dinah lay back on the grass and flowers. The smell of the earth tickled her senses. She felt reborn, as though the heavens had opened. The sky and the clouds on the horizon seemed to be dancing just for them. "You asked me if I had ever made love on a forest floor. I said no. I've never made love in a meadow full of wild flowers either, but I'm willing to try." She turned to face him. "I think I'm falling in love with you, too and I'm sorry you had to almost die for me to realize it."

Nero sucked in a deep breath and pulled her close. "There is nothing I would rather do than make love to you on a meadow or anywhere else…but you didn't say quite the right words." He pushed her away. "I know a lot more about you now and I can wait for them…without the qualifiers."

Dinah pretended outrage. "What? I finally throw myself at you and look what happens." She smiled through her tears. "You're alive, let's get out of here."

Nero rose to his feet.

"Wait," She pulled him back down. "I have to tell you something, something bad." She drew up her knees and hugged them. "Back there, those men. I could have easily killed them. I wanted to kill them. If nothing else, I hurt them quite badly." She grimaced. "Maybe I'm the evil twin. Maybe my brother knew it and that's why he tried to smother me as a child."

"Dinah! Listen to me. You didn't kill them, but you could have, you just said so. That speaks volumes. Don't go back and rehash it." He shook her shoulder. "Professor Dumas recognized the good in you and so do I. One more time, I love you."

"Okay," she replied, but she still trembled at the recollection of her actions, and she still couldn't tell him the words he wanted to hear.

CHAPTER NINE

Colonel Preston fidgeted on the hard bench outside Command Headquarters. The time had come to pay the price, even though a moron could determine it was not his squad's fault the mission failed. But you don't screw up or get second chances when it comes to serving the president. Several times last night he'd considered eating his pistol as an honorable solution but changed his mind when an alternative suggested itself in his cold and calculating mind. Revenge. He had never craved it so deeply, and he had craved it often. Men in his family always got the last word. His ex-wife could attest to that.

He glanced at the fierce looking redheaded man in the dark suit who sat near the door. Was he waiting to see someone, too? Surely not the president?

The door swung open and the president's aide, Harold Baxter, exited the office and approached Jake.

"Colonel Preston, sir, the president asked me to tell you he won't be seeing you today." He handed Jake a package. "He asked me to deliver your new assignment."

Without further fanfare, Baxter turned to the tall red haired man with the powerful build. "I assume you are Max Malone?"

The man rose and followed Baxter into the president's temporary office.

So, they had elected to be done with him, Jake guessed, without even the honor of a face-to-face. Well, he would not be discounted so lightly. They would pay, all of them, the flying freaks and maybe even the president and especially the tall creep who had obviously taken his place. Jake had trained his men to follow him not their country. By God, he had his own hand-picked band of assassins. And after the alien struck them down on their mission, his men would relish the idea of following him anywhere to inflict reprisals, which is what he could have offered the president if he had not dismissed him for things beyond his control. *How do you fight super powers?* He would make it his life's work to find out. He tossed the envelope on the side table. He had made out his retirement papers last night, just in case. He'd have a few beers with his men tonight and turn in his resignation first thing in the morning. He'd served long enough and would not end up in bum-fuck anywhere unless he chose to.

Just as he was leaving the door to the office opened once more and two women walked out talking to one another.

"That red headed guy is one creepy dude."

"Yeah, and he has cold dead eyes. Beautiful baby blues shining out to the world, but there's a soulless demon in there. When he smiled at me I felt as though the air had been sucked out of the room." She shivered. "I feel sorry for the person they sic him on."

CHAPTER TEN

Max Malone sat quietly, listening to Harold
Baxter fill in the details of the last few weeks,
from the incident involving the hikers to the
episode last night when Colonel Preston's men
were summarily downed by a flying red-haired
woman. He paid close attention, at the same time
noting details of the room and the other two
people in it. This was no Oval Office, but they
had apparently refurnished it for the president's
visit. No military issue desk for the overweight,
prima donna with the wavy blond hair who sat
regally enthroned behind the polished mahogany

desk. Heavy brass lamps lit the room with soft lighting, and a decanter of fine brandy sat on a side table.

"Any questions?" Baxter asked.

Yeah, Max thought, what rock did they dig you out from under? "Certainly," he said aloud, "The most important of which is how many people besides Preston's squad are aware of the particulars regarding what has transpired to date. I would like a list, if you don't mind. Of everyone involved."

The aide rolled his eyes as if to indicate dismissal. "Preston's crew members all have top-secret clearance. You needn't worry on that score."

Max narrowed his eyes and spoke forcefully, to make sure the geeky blond aide grasped who made the decisions. "From now on, I'll be the judge of who knows what—and how to handle them."

The president sat upright. "Are you suggesting eliminating Preston's squad?" The president asked. He quickly raised both hands in the air. "Wait. Never mind, you're absolutely right, it's your mission, Max, and you have always done what needed to be done." He turned his face to the far wall. "For that matter, even I don't have a need to know, so don't tell me your plans except for when they deal with capturing these ah…super beings. We need to harness their power before someone else does. It's for the good of the country!" He looked at his aide. "You're excused, Harold."

"And keep your trap shut, Harold." Max added. "Or your name goes on my list."

The chagrined aide left without a word, but a dark scowl shadowed his face.

"This may take some doing, Mr. President." Max never said, sir, to anyone. "It's important to learn everything about the enemy before striking prematurely as Preston did. And you needn't worry about other powers getting to the aliens first. Word will not get out."

The president stood. "That would be comforting, were it true. You've seen the newspapers and the television coverage of that boy. The whole world knows."

"The best way to cover a leak is to incorporate it, not bury it. We'll need some of the top secret personal-rocket technology they've been playing with out in the desert. We stick one on a red haired woman, let her be seen flying it, and say it was part of an exercise. That's a lot more believable than what's in the newspaper now." He moved to the door. "I've already set the plan in motion. It should be tomorrow's headlines."

The president laughed and sat back down. "I knew I could count on you, Max. Do what you have to do." He waved him toward the door.

"One more thing," Max said, turning. "I can do a lot of things, but computer hacking is not one of them. Get that geeky aide of yours to find out who is running the superhero website." He slammed the door behind him.

Max stopped at Harold's desk. Something bothered him, something from his distant past, a story he'd heard as a child maybe, he couldn't pin it down, but it concerned a place with a portal or a pool. The trekker story had triggered the recollection.

"A map, of where the hikers were first spotted, I want it." he said to Baxter. "I'll wait while you burn a copy. And make it quick."

He already knew where to find the Colonel and his pals. They were stupidly predictable. Gyms and bars, an unlikely combination, but one invariably led to the other. A good workout called for a cold beer—the routine of macho men. But what the heck, everyone deserved a cold beer before dying. Tonight would work.

CHAPTER ELEVEN

Dinah relaxed on the third floor balcony of the mansion enjoying the view of the sea. She watched schools of fish jumping outside the reef as predators herded them. Except for the hammering of construction workers, the private key was the next best thing to Heaven.

Two weeks had passed since their escape from the forest, but Dinah still had problems when she remembered the incident. Nero insisted her treatment of the soldiers was what anyone would have done if they had her powers. The problem, as she perceived it was–they didn't–and she did. She also wondered if she were capable of worse, and inwardly acknowledged the answer. The fact that the soldiers all died in a bar fight a day later, didn't lessen her guilt. According to the paper, only one had survived. She'd studied his picture to make certain he wasn't one of the men she had rendered unconscious. Apparently, he was their leader and he was now AWOL. The bar brawl suggested personal implications, which didn't explain why he went into hiding. *Was he hiding from her?*

There was no point in continuing her analysis of what it all meant, she had more important issues to consider. Mr. Lau had called to say he would arrive around noon today. She had made it her business to see to the cabin he would occupy. With the help of an online decorator, and Rafael's on the computer, she had ordered elegant oriental decor from a catalog. The assistant assured her Lau would like it.

She couldn't wait to begin furnishing the three other cabins set aside for his family, especially after Lau told her his granddaughters might choose American modern styles.

Lau had originally declined their offer to move to the compound, firmly resolved to conduct business as usual until he could afford to bring his family to America. When Nero informed him of their plan to import his family for free as part of the deal, he nearly bowed himself to the floor professing gratitude. It brought tears to Dinah's eyes. Thereupon, they agreed to make arrangements to bring his sister, nephew and two granddaughters, promising all would be paid handsomely for helping to maintain the mansion and grounds. Mr. Lau quickly sold his small apartment, and the family would soon follow with Rafael's diplomatic machinations on their behalf.

Rafael tapped on the sliding glass doors before joining her on the balcony. "Some interesting developments on the website this morning, though I've had to shift its base several times, it seems someone is trying to track us down. But we knew that would be happening sooner or later."

"So we're safe from detection?"

He shrugged. "I feel confident we've avoided the worst. I did get a letter from the father of the boy you saved. He wanted you to know a man with a badge, a very large red haired man, came around asking questions. The father also said the agent spent more than an hour grilling him and when it finally ended, he suspected the man had considered killing him. Seriously, he said that were it not for the television announcing another sighting of the superheroes, he believed the man would have enjoyed killing him. Pure evil, is how he described him. He's quite shaken up. Basically, he sent the email to warn you about this guy."

"You think it's my long lost brother, don't you, Rafe?"

"And you don't? Get real." Rafe dropped into the nearest chair and poured himself some lemonade from the pitcher on the table.

"First of all, I didn't have red hair until the pool incident, so what makes you sure my brother does? Am I going to have to fear every person on the planet with red hair?"

"Don't be silly, I was thinking more along the lines of the description of him as 'pure evil.' The professor used similar words to describe him."

Dinah leaned against the chair back and sighed. "How's the rest of the email sorting coming along?"

"I've put in some filters, which helped. Although I received two messages this morning, one I want to follow up on, and the other I want you to check out carefully. I'm afraid the website may serve as a channel for them to draw you out. It started out as a good idea, but we may have to shut it down and settle for a Google alert on selected news items."

"You're the expert. Those decisions belong to you." Dinah leaned forward. "Tell me about the call you believe to be real."

"It's from a little girl who used her

friend's computer to write to you. She said she and her little sister want to go home to their mommy, but their grandmother won't let them. She gave me the name of the town and the street they live on. She described the house as dirty brown brick, with two big trees out front and a big star over the front door."

Dinah straightened. "What color is the star? A blue star usually denotes a family member is serving on the front, and a gold star means the soldier died in action. The Blue Star and Gold Star Mothers have been recognized for their devotion to all veterans since WWII, and they send them gifts and welcome them home."

"Oh, oh, she mentioned a gold star. She also said they were hungry because their grandmother wouldn't feed them for a whole day if they mentioned their mother."

He shook his head. "The problem is that I'm not sure we should get involved in a family dispute, other than to notify the authorities we suspect mistreatment of the children."

Dinah heard activity below and walked to

the balcony railing. She leaned out, inhaling the aroma of Jasmine and lime blossoms. The rattle of a rickety bus approaching by way of their little bridge caught her immediate attention.

"Mr. Lau is coming! I can't wait for him to see his new home." She turned back to Rafael. "About the children, I have an idea. Nero and I will locate the house and find out who lives there and then you can get on your trusty computer and find out everything about them." She grinned. "And this means I get to wear my new costume! Yeehaw!"

"You are such a child!" Rafael laughed. "How does Nero put up with you? Now I know why he calls you a goof-ball."

"Oh, come on!" She grabbed him by the hand and pulled him toward the sliding glass doors. "Let's go down and welcome Mr. Lau, you will love him."

"Okay, okay! He sighed. "And I reluctantly agree that tonight you check out the child's house. Late tonight."

CHAPTER TWELVE

With a great deal of practice, Dinah had mastered the art of comfortably taking Nero with her when she flew. She found she could simply hold his hand and he could fly beside her rather than clinging to her body as he had done previously. It required some convincing to get him to try the new method, but once they were successful, he was all for it.

"I thought about pretending to almost fall," he confessed, "so I could go back to wrapping myself around your gorgeous body.

Flying practically glued together raises my erotic impulses to a new level."

Dinah glanced over at him as they neared the small town's clock tower. "It so happens I've noticed how much you enjoyed it." She jabbed him in the ribs. "I see it as a recipe for a mid-air collision."

"I like the sound of that." He laughed. "Hmm…having your fans see you flying is one thing, what I had in mind is quite another. Wouldn't the tabloids love a little porno on their cover? And have I mentioned, your suit is magnificent? Lau is a true craftsman." He squeezed her hand. "Isn't this where women usually say, 'Does this outfit make me look fat?'"

"Oh, hush up." She glanced sideways at him and frowned, "Does it? And don't answer that or I'll drop you." She zeroed in on the houses below, hoping to match the girl's description. It didn't take long.

"I'm going to circle from a distance and see if I can spot one of the girls' bedrooms."

"Why didn't Rafe just email her and ask

her name and address?"

Dinah understood his confusion on the subject. "She sent the message through someone else's email account and he decided the less interaction on the Internet, the better. Besides, he assumed we could find out." She stopped behind the line of trees surrounding the property. Narrowing her eyes, she zoomed in for details. "Bunk beds," she whispered, "top floor, last window toward the rear. It has to be their room. I'm going to leave you here for a minute," she said. "Think you'll be okay in a tree?"

"Make darn sure I have a secure position before you let go…please"

Dinah peered through the dust encrusted window and evaluated the situation. The only furnishings in the room consisted of the bunk beds and one large dresser. She had expected to see toys scattered about, even a stuffed animal or two, but spotted none. Also missing were the normal little girl accoutrements, frilly bedspreads, or posters of pop stars on the walls. It could pass for a military barracks. As she stared at the sleeping children, it hit her. Both had one foot out from under the covers—because they were tethered to the bed by ropes. The children were prisoners in their own beds.

Dinah returned to the tree and Nero. "What should we do?" She asked him after revealing the details of what she had seen. Tears streamed down her face.

Nero kissed them away. "What's your gut feeling?"

"I want to snatch them right out of there and then I want to go back in, grab dear old Granny and tie her to the nearest light post with a sign around her neck that reads, *child abuser*!"

Nero chuckled. "That's what I love about you, your ability to make sensible decisions under stress." He leaned back against the trunk of the tree. "Okay, I'm with you, but how do we get in. Do we do a Superman routine, turn on our e-ray vision and burn a hole through the side of the house?"

"A lot of people don't lock their upstairs windows assuming thieves can't scale straight up the walls. Not everyone flies, you know."

"Oh, yeah, I know. First you need to get the children out; then you go back and deal with Granny. Agreed? And put me on the ground so I can watch them."

Dinah's adrenaline pounded in her ears. At last some superhero action for a good cause. She helped Nero to the ground and returned to the window. She could see the lock was unlatched and gave a sigh of relief. As gently as she could she slid it up and stepped into the room. The eerie glow of moonlight cast strange shadows in the corners. The child in the top bunk moved, probably alerted by the breeze now wafting through the open window. Her eyes suddenly opened and expanded into saucers as she spied Dinah. She opened her mouth to scream, but stifled it when Dinah signaled to her by raising one finger to her lips.

"I'm here about your email," she

whispered. "I'm going to take you away to a secret place and we will find your mommy." She approached the bed and untied the rope from the girl's ankle.

"Ouch, that hurts," the girl said.

Even in the dim moonlight, Dinah could see the raw skin encircling her ankle. She drew in slow deep breaths to calm herself, remembering how her anger had affected her with the soldiers. It wouldn't do to kill Grandma, although the urge to, simmered.

"We need to wake your little sister. Do you want to do it?" She asked assisting the child off the bed. "What's your name?"

"It's Annie, but we can't wake Lily, Granny gives her drugs to make her sleep, because she cries a lot."

It required a herculean effort not to race out of the room and throttle Granny.

"We're going to leave now, I'll come right back for you sister. Okay?"

Annie busied herself untying Lily. "No! I won't leave without Lily."

Dinah started to explain but was interrupted by a noise from downstairs. Footsteps sounded in the distance. Someone climbed the stairs.

A harsh voice called out. "What's all the chatter up there?"

Dinah helped Annie fight with the rough cord holding Lily to the bed. "Quickly," she instructed Annie, "Climb on my back, I'll carry Lily."

Annie hesitated. "What if I fall?"

"I won't let you fall. Just hold on tight. Hurry!"

The footsteps reached the door and Dinah heard a key in the lock. Not only did the woman tie the children up and drug them, she locked them in. The thought of children trapped in a house-fire crossed Dinah's mind. Granny deserved the worst. With Annie clinging to her back, she scooped Lily into her arms, raced for the window, and stepped onto the roof. She inhaled the stale odor of cigarettes and booze as the door opened and Granny walked in and screamed at the top of her lungs.

"Give me back my babies! I'll kill you, you bitch!"

The hag's words followed Dinah across the open space between the house and the trees. It tore at her heart to hear Annie sobbing against her back.

After she settled the children and assured them Nero would watch out for them until she came back, she turned to the ugly brown brick house.

Dinah entered through the same window only to find Granny had disappeared. She opened the bedroom door and called out to her. "Oh, Granny, I'm baaaaccck......

CHAPTER THIRTEEN

Dinah fought the rage bubbling below the surface of her mind. Granny deserved her fate, she thought, but then, who made her judge of that fate? She dug deeply to summon up the memory of the expressions of abject fear on the faces of the soldiers in the moments before she stunned them. They would never know or understand how their reflected terror influenced the rest of their lives, because in a split-second, the choice of killing or stunning them presented itself as

148

clearly as a three-dimensional vision, one that made Dinah choose her left fist over her right. The opposite selection would have been fatal. She clung firmly to that thought now as she slipped out the bedroom door in search of Granny, her right fist tucked tightly against her hip, but the knowledge of the extent of her power would linger and fester. Having super powers did not bestow tranquility, it came with heavy burdens, burdens only a discerning conscience could manage.

She traveled the dark hallway to the top of the stairs and focused her eyes to search the deep corners of the lower floor. Her concentration paid off, because she discovered she could now see perfectly in the dark. A new power to add to her already impressive arsenal.

She heard and felt Granny's presence behind her in the seconds before the woman struck, leaping onto her back like a feral cat. The crazed woman tried to sink her teeth into Dinah's neck as they tumbled forward into space, but Mr. Lau's metallic suit prevented her from succeeding.

Dinah didn't bother to fight back, instead she moved them from the top of the stairs to the open space above the living room below.

Granny suddenly loosened her grip and whipped her head in all directions, apparently realizing they were suspended in mid-air.

"Lord, have mercy! You're an agent of the devil come to make me pay for my sins. Dear, God," she continued in her whiskey tenor. "I'm heartily sorry for having offended thee by what I have done…but I loved them, Lord, I lost my babies."

Dinah felt hot tears drop onto her shoulders, and gently settled Granny to the ground. She didn't understand, but that's not why she was here. She had rescued the girls; she would leave Granny's fate to her God and the local police. With a heavy sigh, she pushed the weeping woman into the nearest chair and marched out the front door.

~*~

Dinah slept soundly, but something, perhaps a new sense of awareness that came with her other super powers, woke her. The noise was barely audible, like a rustling of material, and it came from somewhere near the floor. The next thing she heard was the bloodcurdling screams of two small children as they launched themselves from the floor at the foot of her bed and landed beside her.

Their giggles were irrepressible and Dinah added hers to the cacophony.

"Did Nero put you up to this? She asked, knowing full well he had.

"Yes!" Annie shouted, "And guess what, Mr. Zappy found our mommy."

"Mr. Zappy, huh? His name is really Zapata, but I like your version better."

"Okay," Annie said, "But Zappy said you need to get downstairs fast, people are here."

"People?" Dinah felt a tightness in her throat. *Mr. Lau kept close watch on the gate to the bridge, how had people gotten by him?* He

151

hadn't sounded the alarm. *Was the enemy in their camp?* She threw her feet over the side of the bed, ready for action. "Tell Zappy I'm on my way! Quickly now, I have to get dressed."

~*~

The people turned out to be Mr. Lau's family. She found them in the kitchen, loudly proclaiming the virtues of the Viking appliances as they stroked them lovingly. There were two girls, women really, one of which was the most stunning creature Dinah had ever seen. She was taller than most Asians by a foot, and her complexion was right out of Elle. Beyond her striking looks, was the way she held herself, like a queen. The younger woman was perfectly lovely, too, but paled in comparison. She grinned mightily at Dinah and bowed. Mr. Lau introduced the beauty as Trinh and her sister as Mai. Everyone bowed, and bowed and bowed, Dinah noticed, everyone except for *Zappy* that is, who chose this occasion to act *sappy* and stood frozen in place as he gawked at Trinh. Dinah elbowed him in the ribs and he finally joined the real world once more, and bowed.

Lau waved one hand toward the door "Others outside to look at sea. Sister, Lynh, and grandson, Danh. Come, I introduce."

Once the family was settled in their respective cabins, Dinah turned to Rafael. "What was that all about? Are you smitten with the woman?"

"Don't be ridiculous!" He protested strongly. "Anyway, I'm glad you're up, Nero went to town for extra supplies for our new guests, lots of rice, bamboo shoots, dried fish and a whole bunch of other stuff I've never even heard of."

Dinah poured herself a cup of coffee from the silver urn. "The girls said you found their mother, is that true?"

Rafe sat down across from her at the table. He ran his hand over its smooth surface. "I seem to remember a table like this." His eyes reflected that distant quality Dinah now recognized. It usually proceeded one of his brooding moods which was followed by a full day in his room, writing.

"Yes," he finally answered. "I put the girls' pictures on the Internet this morning and almost instantly received a response from a small town in Ohio. The sheriff said he'd fielded a dozen phone calls just minutes after the pictures appeared. Apparently the whole world looks at the site hourly. You and Nero get more hits than the lottery." He smiled broadly, dispersing the gloom from moments before. "I asked the girls where they wanted to meet their mother. Obviously, we can't have her come here. Guess where?" He raised an eyebrow. "You're going to love this!"

CHAPTER FOURTEEN

Max stood on the trail above the pool and stared. He felt something tug at his body and looked up trying to locate the source of his discomfort. Yes, this was the right place, the place where super powers were born, he knew it instinctively.

A small dense cloud hovered in the distance. At first it appeared to be expanding, but he soon realized it wasn't growing, it was moving—moving toward him. A smattering of goose bumps rose on his forearms, and his scalp tingled. He turned and tried to run but the cloud followed. He lost his footing for a minute and clutched at nearby trees and their exposed roots. He fell and the lightning struck his heel, and although pain ricocheted throughout his whole body, it passed momentary. He clung to the bushes with all his might until the pull diminished.

Max remained in place for thirty minutes, exhausted, trying to understand the significance of what had happened. He inhaled a deep breath, and instantly distinguished a thousand odors at one time. His sense of smell suddenly rivaled that of a hunting dog. He laughed aloud. He *was* a hunting dog, a killer wolf, if the truth be known. As super powers went, an intense sense of smell might not be the most desirable attribute, but it also may not be the only one he now possessed. Experimenting would be exciting.

He thought back to the removal of Preston's squad and reveled in the moment. Blood sports were his favorite. Preston had escaped, but Max would ultimately remedy that glitch. He closed his eyes and sniffed, funny, he could even smell in retrospect. He now had Preston's scent in his olfactory archive.

Max sat up. Maybe he could do the same with the memories of his sister, the bitch. He could still remember everyone fawning over her night and day, and ignoring him. He closed his eyes again and pictured himself leaning over her bed. He saw her long blond curls spread out on the pillow. Loathing stuck like a bullet. In his recollection he remembered snatching the pillow from under her and placing it over her too pretty face. He sucked in air trying to capture her essence as he had Preston's, but each time he did, what he smelled instead was the sense of horror emanating from his father as he roughly picked him up and pinned him against the wall. Face to face, he saw the love-light he so desperately craved, flicker and die in his father's eyes.

Max panted with rage at himself, rage at his inability to strike back. If they could see me now, he thought, all of his family, they wouldn't dare dismiss me quite so easily. I'd render them into dog food. Literally. But forget them, it was his sister he really wanted, the root of his abandonment, and he was absolutely certain the missing trekker named Dinah and his sister were one and the same.

~*~

The phone call stunned Jake Preston and he couldn't believe his luck. He sat propped on a barstool in a cantina in Mexico. It briefly occurred to him to wonder how Harold Baxter had gotten his private cell number. Under other circumstances the information might have given him pause, but this might be fortuitous.

For days after Max Malone killed his men, Jake had plotted revenge. The aliens took a back seat to his desire to destroy Malone, but Baxter's call changed everything. Apparently Max had threatened the wrong person when he singled out Harold, but people who imagined themselves invulnerable often made the mistake of underestimating their enemies. Harold may not be macho, but he was cunning and he was smart. He hadn't risen to his position in Washington on his charm.

Harold shared his thoughts with Jake on the phone. "The president may not want to know Malone's agenda, but I do, and I've set a course designed to cover our asses. Max has marked us both for elimination and unless we get to him first, he will succeed, but first he wants to capture the aliens, which I promise you will be his undoing."

Jake considered the possibility that this might be a ruse to get him, dreamed up by Harold. But the story rang true and he had nothing to lose by listening. "I'm with you so far."

"Max plans to set a trap for the new superheroes. Along with half the country, he went to their website and thinks he knows what might bring them straight to his chosen battlefield. If small children with problems draw them like bees to honey, he'll build them a hive."

"So, why call me? And what's all this

superhero talk?" Jake sipped his cold beer and rested one elbow on the bar.

After a moment's hesitation, Harold answered. "As for calling you, don't be offended, but you and I have different talents. I'm the brains and you're the brawn. You're fearless, to boot. I'm not, but I have the good sense to know it."

Jake recalled Harold's slight frame, fair hair and delicate hands. No, he wouldn't do well in a fire-fight. Not the kind of soldier you'd want to have your back. But as a strategist, he did have the requisite manipulative mind. Learning Max's plans was proof of that. Perhaps they would make a good team.

He signaled the bartender. *"Uno mas cerveza por favor."* To Harold Baxter he said, "I'm in. What's the plan? I want to get those aliens though."

Harold laughed softly. "I thought you might, but that's another issue. You asked about superheroes, when's the last time you heard the national news?" He didn't wait for an answer.

"Obviously you haven't, so I'll fill you in. Our alien superheroes have been up to good deeds again, but for my part I don't give a shit about them."

"Hey, they hurt my men."

"No—you're wrong. Max Malone hurt your men, permanently. The aliens could have, I believe, but instead they removed them from action while they escaped, and then, only after being attacked first."

Jake grunted in reply. "We'll argue the details later, in the meantime, tell me what heroic acts you've observed."

"I didn't observe them. Anyway, according to the television news hawks, they rescued two small children who were abducted a year ago. Seems some old lady's son came home from the war and found his wife with another man. He went berserk and blew her and his kids away; then he killed himself."

"Yeah, so?"

"So, the soldier's mother traded her blue star for a gold one and hung it in her window, then snatched herself some new grandchildren. Poor little things weren't too fond of Granny, and didn't make nice like she wanted. She resorted to tying them up at night so they wouldn't run away. Worse yet, she didn't feed them half the time. The kids sent an email to the superheroes and, *Shazam*, they race to the rescue. Hell, they'll probably make a movie about it, the kids are so cute. Once their pictures hit the Internet, their mother surfaced faster than Nellie at Loch Ness. The heroes delivered them in broad daylight by flying them to Disney World where Mom picked them up. It was one hell of a show. Poor Granny missed it, she ended up in a psych unit, but the tears of millions are still flowing on *YouTube*."

"Damn," Jake couldn't believe it. Still, if not for the aliens, or superheroes as they were now calling them, he would still be working for the president of the United States, not hanging out in some hovel in the middle of nowhere. They might not be on Harold's list, but they remained near the top of his.

Harold cleared his throat. "I'll call you as

soon as I know what Max's plan is, but you need to come back in-country and be ready. Let's get the bastard!" He hung up.

CHAPTER FIFTEEN

Nero and Dinah snuggled in the hammock. "All right," Nero said, "I've decided the torture should end. You agreed to make love in a meadow and I turned you down for my own stubborn reasons. Well, I've changed my mind; I want you so badly I can no longer sleep for imagining how it will be to make love to you. I want to see your face in the throes of passion." He slid his hand around her back to pull her closer. "So, how do you feel about making love in a hammock, since there are no meadows or forest floors to be found on a coral island?" He looked into her eyes. "Or we can go to my room. Or yours?"

Dinah started to reply, but he placed one finger to her lips.

"Wait, don't answer that. Let me work on persuading you first."

He kissed her hard and long, the whole while letting his hands explore her body, driving her mad with wanting him. She felt his desire and matched it, trying not to think of the dreams that haunted her since her encounter with the girls' pseudo grandmother. She had to let it go. She closed her eyes reveling in Nero's exploration. But the memory came rushing back."

"I can't!" She bellowed. "Because I'm a monster." She unwound herself from his embrace and jumped from the hammock. "Don't you see? I could have happily killed that sick old lady, only her pathetic prayers stopped me." She stepped back so he couldn't reach her. "Besides, even if I never kill anyone, the potential is there, it's in my genes. The aliens…Dumma…they're right! We shouldn't mate. Our children might turn out even worse than my brother and me!"

She turned and ran to the mansion.

~*~

Nero found Dinah in her room, sitting quietly near the window.

"Here's the deal," he said. "I love you and I will never believe you are a monster of any kind. As for children, we have two choices, never have any, or adopt. Problem solved. I'll take my chances, because I can't live without you."

Dinah threw herself into his arms. "Give me time, just give me time."

"How does forever sound? I give you forever and ever."

~*~

"Dinah! Nero!" Rafe shouted from outside the door.

Nero sprang into action. He raced to the door and flung it open. "For God's sake, what is it? You sound panicked."

"The professor, he wrote to the website!"

"But that's wonderful!" Dinah exclaimed. She spied the paper in his hand and reached for it. "Let me have it."

She carried it over to her desk, sat down and read it aloud.

~*~

Dearest Dinah,

I knew the moment those men came to my door their visit would concern you. And I knew from their questions you had found the portal. By now, you will have emptied the deposit box and know a great deal more about yourself and me. I hope you do not choose to hate me for my part in all of this.

Because the tsars keep spies in place around the planet, they immediately suspected your origin. They do not expect you will accept their invitation, but they would like you to pay a visit to the lower world, which we call, Sapphire after our home planet. You would be warmly welcomed as we are not a cruel or vindictive race. I, of course, had no recourse but to return as my usefulness on Earth is at an end. I can and will contact you as often as possible. The burning question for me and the tsars right now concerns the man who accompanies you on your missions of mercy. They call him, Nero. Surely he is not your twin, Max? And if not, from where did he acquire his powers? But back to Max, he will now hunt you down, on this point all are agreed. I have said we are not a cruel race, but he must be destroyed before he discovers he too may possess unknown powers.

My love....your Dumma

~*~

Dinah looked up from the page with resolve. She nodded at Nero. "Don't give it a thought, I'm not going. That pool scares the hell out of me, and since I'm not fully one of them, I might not be able to make it to the bottom, I could drown. And as for the other part, I can't destroy anyone. I mean I can, but I don't want to. To be more specific, how do you kill your own twin?"

"You don't," Rafe declared. He looked at Nero, "We do. But that's a conversation for Nero and I to have in private. About going to Sapphire, I don't think you should dismiss the idea so lightly. The professor wouldn't suggest it if he thought you might come to harm."

Dinah wrapped her arms across her chest and shuddered. "I don't want to even think about it right now." She stared into his eyes. "Read my lips, Rafe. I will not go!"

Rafe nodded. "Okay, I can see how much the prospect frightens you. The invitation must be addressed sooner or later, however. Seriously.

"By the way, there is another letter like

the one last week. It's from someone claiming to have information about children being held captive in a compound, one of those religious cults. The author of the letter says they are forcing children as young as ten years old to perform sexual acts with the elders."

"This is the story you suspect to be a trap, isn't it?" Nero asked.

"Yes," Rafe sat down in Dinah's recliner and leaned back, then looked startled when the foot rest sprang out. "Hey, I want one of these. Anyway, the reason I think it may not be true is because I had an investigator go there and interview half the town. According to him, the cult mingles with the townspeople constantly and the cult invites the public to visit unrestricted and openly at all times. If there is something secret going on it might just be in this guy's twisted imagination. Or, I as I suspect, it's a trap. There is a tunnel involved, that's just one thing about it that worries me."

Dinah nodded. "Yes, but cults are notorious for keeping their baser practices hidden. You know that old adage, sometimes the best way to hide…is in plain sight. What exactly does the person writing suggest we do?"

"He claims to have been a member and says all the hanky-panky goes on in the night in an underground chamber, but he knows a secret way into the chamber, the tunnel I spoke of, and claims he can lead us through it to see for ourselves."

"Hmmm…" Nero sat propped against Dinah's headboard. "If all we have to do is look, where's the harm?"

Rafe sat up straighter. "Because, don't you get it? I don't want you caught in a tunnel, you'll be trapped. Only bats fly out of tunnels."

Dinah paced the room. "Ohhh…I see what you mean. But, if it's true what they're doing to those children, it's awful." She stopped and faced Nero. "I say we have no choice but to check it out."

CHAPTER SIXTEEN

Jake and Harold met the in food-court of Melody Mall at lunchtime so as to blend in with the teaming throngs of shoppers.

"You're looking happier than the last time I saw you," Harold said, shaking his hand.

Jake resisted the urge to wipe his hand on his trousers. Harold always left him feeling slimy after an encounter. He'd dealt with two-faced men several times in his line of work, usually they were simple snitches, but even he knew Harold hadn't made it to the office of the president as a petty informant. He would bet there were bodies buried beneath the ladder of his success.

"According to my source, Max has funneled irresistible information to our superheroes. He has them believing they are going to rescue dozens of children from a sex-crazed cult." He crossed his arms over his chest and let out a belly laugh. "It's too perfect. I told you he would build them a hive. I may not like this guy, but that doesn't mean I don't admire his panache."

Jake had no clue what the fuck *panache* meant, but he would never ask this little prick. He kept checking out the nearby customers, concerned one might recognize him from the newspaper photos, even though Harold had assured him that he looked totally different out of uniform, especially with a baseball cap on. But Harold was Harold and not to be trusted, Christ, the man turned traitor on the president himself. "Obviously, you have a place for me in this scenario. Let's cut to the heart of the plan." He glanced around again. "I don't appreciate meeting in public."

"Quit worrying, I've got you covered." Harold sipped soda from a straw and dipped a nacho in cheese sauce."

Jake struck like a rattler, grabbing Harold's outstretched hand in a vice-like grip. "Maybe you came here for lunch, I didn't, cough up the plan."

"Hey, don't get your panties in a wad."

Jake twisted Harold's wrist to one side.

"Sweet Jesus! Let go!"

Jake loosened his grip and Harold snatched his arm away. He absently rubbed it as he outlined the attack on Dinah and Nero. "They will arrive at the site around midnight. I'm supposed to lead them into the tunnel, which has no exit, by the way. Max had it specially dug for the occasion, installed lights, the whole works. The superheroes have been told it's a getaway tunnel for the cult.

"Once inside, Max plans to capture them by sealing the entrance. He told the president they would be gassed into unconsciousness and brought to a government lab for testing." He smiled. "Between you and me, I think he has special plans for the woman. I know he has an armored vehicle standing by that's not on the equipment list for the mission. My money says he hands them the guy and claims the woman got clean away. It's her he really wants for some reason."

"And where do we come in?"

"Like I said, I deliver the gas for the mission. You'll want to be nearby for this, I'll need your help for the final phase. Bring your gun."

"Okay, so you gas the aliens, then you want me to shoot Max?"

"Noo…I let Max think I gassed the aliens, but what I use will just look like gas. Smoke and mirrors, you know the drill. So he goes in and then I gas them all, with poisonous gas though, no foo-foo stuff. The gun is for back-up, in case the gas doesn't work on the aliens."

Forgetting he wasn't alone for a minute, Jake slammed his palm down on the table. "Holy shit, nice plan

CHAPTER SEVENTEEN

"I still don't like the idea, it has all the markings of a trap," Rafael protested. "I may not have Nero's keen sense of danger, but a child could see through this one." He stood near the balcony window with his back to them while Dinah and Nero put on their costumes.

Dinah smoothed her already smooth, skin-tight metallic suit. "Nevertheless, it comes to the same thing every time we have this discussion—what if it's true and the children need rescuing?" She didn't wait for an answer. "I know, I know. Call the authorities and report our suspicions. But you keep forgetting, the informant says he has done so numerous times to no avail."

Rafe raised both fists in the air. "Exactly, *the informant says!* My investigator insists he spoke with the same authorities and *they say*, there have been no complaints. The inhabitants, the ones who see them every day, love these people."

Nero spoke for the first time since Rafe had entered the room ranting and raving. "Rafe, you can turn around now. We're going. If you have something useful to add, do so." He pointed at Dinah who was donning her mask. "You know how she is when it comes to children. They win all ties, so you may as well give up."

Rafe sighed, walked over, and sat down at Dinah's desk, resignation written on his face. He bent and retrieved something from his bag. "At least add these to your bag of tricks." He extracted two small face masks with small bladders attached. "You won't wear the bullet proof vests I had made for you, and you won't carry guns, so you owe me this much. You don't have to wear them going in, but carry them in your packs, it will make me happy. They're the absolute latest in gas masks and they only weigh a few ounces. They're good for five minutes tops, but it will give you a chance. Look, I figured out what I would do to trap you if I wanted to, and gas is what I came up with. Or a cave-in from an explosion. Think about it. You'll be in a tunnel, for crying out loud." He frowned. "I wish I hadn't thought of explosives! I can't protect you from bombs."

Dinah walked over to Rafe and hugged him. "We'll be careful, now stop worrying."

The moonless night worked to their advantage, allowing them to circle the area unseen before landing at the agreed upon spot. Dinah detected numerous life-forms in the woods surrounding the purported cave entrance, several of them human. She gave the informant credit for having a little back-up, but did consider someone might be watching the informant. She noted three people, one of them very large—in height and girth.

The informant introduced himself as Harold. He was fair-haired and appeared to be in his late thirties, but he fidgeted so much she feared he might not be right in the head. *Had they answered the call of a lunatic?*

"Son, get hold of yourself." Nero warned.

"Sorry, sir, I've just never met real superheroes before. I...I saw you flying and it shook me."

"We're exposed here, let's get to that tunnel," Dinah interrupted. "I'm starting to get nervous myself, it's contagious." She smiled to reassure him.

"Yes, ma'am," he snapped to attention. "Follow me. It's hidden in the side of the hill." He pointed and moved off at a fast pace.

Nero, touched Dinah's shoulder. "I'm sensing something, but it feels different from the vibes I normally pick up. It's something powerful, and I don't know why, but I feel it's hate. Lots of hate and resentment. Do you think it could be coming from the compound? I feel fear, too, but that's rolling off our little guide, like a wave. He's scared silly."

"Keep *reaching*, the whole thing registers as off to me. But it's probably Rafe's influence. He has me looking for boogey men."

Harold stopped in front of a mass of bushes, and pushed them aside one by one until he uncovered a door built into the side of the hill.

Dinah glanced at Nero and nodded. "So far, all things are as advertised."

Nero leaned close to her ear. "I say we take Rafe's advice and have the masks at the ready."

The door opened on squeaky hinges, testimony to infrequent use, or poor maintenance. *Or grit placed on the hinges*, Dinah thought.

Harold stepped inside the entrance and flicked on the lights.

"This is some escape tunnel," Nero remarked, clearly amazed at the quality of the work involved. "The cult must have engineers and limitless funds. The compound probably holds a palace."

Harold stopped. "Oops. I should have pulled the door closed before I hit the switch, we're letting out too much light." Harold quickly stepped around Dinah and Nero, and made as though to close it, but instead slipped out and slammed it behind him.

Nero wasted one hard body slam to the door; then turned to Dinah. "If I turn off the lights, do you think you could see in the dark again, like you did at Granny's?"

"Try it, I don't think we have much time."

Nero hit the switch. "Dinah?"

"Yes! I can do it. But they can just turn the lights back on."

Nero did just that, then bent down and picked up a huge rock and smashed the switch until there was nothing left of it. "Now they can't. Ready or not, prepare for my sparks." He stretched out his hand in the darkness.

Dinah grasped it. "I don't smell gas. Do

you think Rafe was right? Should we activate them? He said we would only have five minutes worth of good air once we do."

"Then we wait for a sound or an odor, or worst scenario, a funny feeling—then we put them on. In the meantime, let's find out what's at the other end of this tunnel."

They had only gone thirty feet around the curved wall when the tunnel came to an abrupt end. It went nowhere. They turned and started back. A hissing noise was their first clue. Gas.

Nero squeezed her hand. "Remember, I can't see. Crouch low and get us to the entrance. Don't don the mask until the last minute. When that door opens I want us to toss the masks as far back inside as we can and play dead. It may take a while for the gas to clear from the rear of the tunnel, so we need to get right up against the door."

Dinah tightened her grip on Nero and raced forward.

"The door is just ahead, but this is close enough. I'm putting the mask on while I still can.

Lie down."

As soon as Dinah felt the rush of fresh air and knew the door had been opened, she removed her mask and stuffed it into her pack, fearing she couldn't throw it far enough that they wouldn't see it. Out of the corner of her eye she saw Nero nod at her and do the same. She heard voices coming their way.

"Turn on the frigging light, asshole."

A sharp scream erupted from Harold.

Dinah could tell it was him by his high tone.

"I can't, they've smashed the switch. The wires shocked me."

"Give me your flashlight."

"Get your own! I'm not going in there in the dark."

A muzzle flash followed and Harold screamed.

"I asked you nicely, now I'll just take it."

Dinah watched the silhouette of the huge man bend over and pick up the flashlight. She also saw someone else enter the cave, someone else carrying a gun, but he didn't have a chance. A second muzzle flash followed the first and the man went down in a heap.

"We'll, look who joined us. Sorry about that, Jake," he said to the man writhing on the ground.

"Fuck you, Max." He fired at the big man, but missed.

Max didn't.

Max turned and started toward Dinah and Nero. "I've been waiting a long time for this, little sister. For years I searched for you after Daddy threw me into foster care."

Dinah felt herself tremble clear down to her toes. Her beloved brother, come to see her at last, stepping over bodies on his way. She wondered how many others he had killed in cold blood over the years. She clenched her fists, feeling the power surge through them. Which should she use to strike back, the left or the right?

Max's flashlight beam found them. "Well, look at you with your flaming red hair. you're even prettier than you were as a child.

When did your hair turn red? Oh, and who have we here, the other superhero. Say goodbye to your lover, Dinah."

Dinah saw him raise his gun and point it at Nero. *Enough.* She and Nero rose at the same time. Dinah raised her fist and a bright blue flash struck Max dead center and he fell like a stone pillar, straight and hard.

"Oh, my God," Dinah said softly, "I've killed my own brother."

"No, you didn't." Nero faced her. "I did."

"But you saw me."

"I saw you raise your arms, but I struck before you could, and I'm not convinced that you would have used your deadly one."

"What are you talking about?"

Nero raised his right arm and made a fist. "Watch." He aimed at the wall and a blue flame shot from his fist and burned a hole in the wall. "I discovered the power yesterday, but I thought maybe it was a one-time occurrence."

"Oh," was all she could think of to say. She hadn't killed her own brother, but still….

She walked over to his body, picked up the flashlight and looked down into his face. She wished she could say he looked peaceful, but he didn't. He looked conflicted. *Was it because in his dying moments he had a hard time believing his own twin could do such a thing to him?* She would never know, but felt comfortable in the fact she actually hadn't. Small consolation, she thought, but knew she would shed no tears either.

Nero led her from the cave. "Let's go home to our little haven in the Keys, and put this all behind us."

Because the whole incident was never reported on the news, Rafael concluded the attack had been organized by the government, and therefore cleaned up by them, as well. "Strange, I would have thought they would try to capture you, not kill you." He said to Dinah and Nero over coffee on the patio behind the mansion.

"Agreed." Nero said. "I believe the plan failed because Max had his own agenda. But enough rehashing the recent past, Dinah and I are leaving today, we're going to take the new identities you provided and go on a much needed vacation."

"It's about time," Rafe exclaimed, clapping Nero on the shoulder.

Nero stood and offered Dinah his arm. "I'd rather we were taking a trek down the aisle, but a trip to an isle will do for now."

~*~

As the airplane lifted off, bound for Hawaii, Dinah reluctantly thought back to that fateful night and the look on her brother's face. She suddenly drew in a sharp breath. "Oh, no!"

"What is it, Dinah? And please don't tell me you're afraid of flying."

"Nero, we've made a terrible mistake."

"Gee, you're just trying to make me feel good, right? And a happy vacation start to you, too!" He laughed.

She rolled her eyes. "Everything isn't

about you," she joked. "But seriously, the expression on Max's face, I've seen it before. I described it as 'conflicted,' but it's the same look you had when I thought you were dead. You know, after you were shot with the dart? I think Max has the same healing power. He was hibernating." Another thought struck her. When Nero hibernated, he could see and hear everything. *Hadn't Nero mentioned their place in the Keys as they left the cave?*

Nero frowned. "No. No way he was hibernating. Max is dead! Come on, Dinah, you're imaging things."

She sighed. "I guess you're right." She kissed him. "Onward!"

The end

I hope you enjoyed my book!
Feel free to contact me at on my guestbook page:

www.JoyceHolland.com

Joyce Holland

Turn the page to read an excerpt from book II of
The Crystal Portal.
Secrets of Sapphire

Secrets of Sapphire

Dinah stood near the edge of the lavender pool and a wave of fear rolled over her like a tsunami. She risked a glance into the deep clear water. *Why had she let Nero and Rafe talk her into this?*

She turned to look at them, hoping for encouragement, or better yet, a reprieve, but saw only her own doubts reflected in their expressions. And they didn't watch *her*, they watched something in the sky. Dinah didn't have to guess what, she could feel it coming—the creepy green cloud she'd spent countless hours avoiding in her dreams. It pulled at her now, and the closer it drew, the stronger its pull. There would be no turning back. *Should she jump into the pool on her own, or wait for the guardians to*

190

throw her in? Either scenario gave her pause, and she shivered in anticipation.

Without warning, time stopped for Dinah and all sound ceased. She tried to turn around, but found herself unable to move as much as a finger. She could no longer see beyond a foot or two. The greenish mist had swallowed her whole.

The mist became a rainbow of colors, colors she could actually feel as they grazed her body gently in passing. They suddenly crystallized around her like a jewel and a sparkling array of facets surrounded her. The jewel made a crackly sound as it solidified.

Dinah felt like bug incased in amber, or a ship in a corked bottle. She could move again, not beyond the confines of the jewel, but within it. Facing Nero once more she noticed she had traveled to a position above the center of the pool—and floated there in her crystal bubble. Below her the water became a whirlpool.

Dinah's fear evaporated, replaced by something else. It wasn't comfort, she realized, it was excitement. She needn't fear drowning on the journey to Sapphire. Dumma would be there for her and who knew what marvels awaited in the world below? She wondered briefly if Nero and Rafe could still see her. She waved and smiled to let them know she was okay.

The jewel began to spin and she had to brace herself against the sides to keep from falling. It went faster and faster until everything outside was a blur. Another minute and she would pass out. Then the crystal dropped Dinah into the lavender abyss that beckoned from the center of the vortex.

"Nooo…" she screamed.

www.ingramcontent.com/pod-product-compliance
Lightning Source LLC
Chambersburg PA
CBHW070916130626
46555CB00001B/156